P9-DMJ-923

Song of the Sparrow

Also by

LISA ANN SANDELL

The Weight of the Sky

Song of the Sparrow

by

LISA ANN SANDELL

SCHOLASTIC PRESS · NEW YORK

An Imprint of Scholastic Inc.

Library of Congress Cataloging-in-Publication Data available

ISBN -13: 978-0-439-91848-0
ISBN -10: 0-439-91848-0

10 9 8 7 6 5 4 3 2 1   07 08 09 10 11
Printed in the U.S.A.
First edition, May 2007

In loving memory of Sydney Sandell

For my two best friends . . .

Sharon, more than you know,

you are a source of inspiration,

of joy and love.

Liel, my partner, my muse,

you are the love and light of my life.

Acknowledgments

Making a book is always so much a collaborative effort, and there are many people who dedicated their time and their talents to getting *Song of the Sparrow* onto the printer's presses. I want to thank my friends and family for being patient while I burrowed away to write, for nourishing me creatively, and, above all, for loving and supporting me.

I must thank my dear friend and editor, Aimee Friedman. Aimee, I do not even know how to begin to thank you properly. You have been a champion, a support, a beacon. Our sparrow could never have grown wings without your guidance and direction, your immense wealth of insight and intuition. You are an incredible editor, a graceful editor, and it has been a tremendous privilege to write for you.

Unending gratitude goes to Charlotte Sheedy, for your invaluable wisdom, boundless care, support, and love; to Meredith Kaffel, for being such a willing and astute reader, for your passionate direction and calm; to my friend, the terrifically talented Elizabeth B. Parisi, for creating a spectacularly beautiful book — I am honored to see my words nestled within your stunning design; and to all of the brilliant people at Scholastic who have given this book life and who have given generously to me over the years their friendship, encouragement, and creative spark: Richard Amari, Dave Barrett, Ellie Berger, Karyn Browne, Susan Jeffers Casel, Margaret Coffee, Jody Corbett, Rachel Coun, Sheila Marie Everett, Nancy Feldman, Susan Flynn, Jacquelyn Fortier, Leslie Garych, Ken Geist, Jacky Harper, Jazan Higgins, Roz Hilden, Lisa Holton, Marijka Kostiw, David Levithan, Mary Marotta, Ed Masessa, John Mason, Charisse Meloto, Suzanne Murphy, Stephanie Nooney, Andrea Pinkney, Arlene Robillard, David Saylor, Francesco Sedita, Alan Smagler, Jill Smith, Courtney Snyder, Tracy van Straaten, Adrienne Vrettos, Elizabeth Whiting, and so many others I have missed — thank you.

And deepest thanks to my parents, for the encouragement and support you show me — I love you so much; to Sharon, my traveling-partner-in-crime and confidante; to Bessie Sandell, for your humor and love; to my Sarahs, Trabucchi and Gelt, for your friendship and love and for being such passionate, insightful readers; to Molly D. Leibovitz, for putting up with all those hours spent at the computer rather than the park; and, finally, to Liel, my first reader and editor, my inspiration, and my very best friend.

Lying, robed in snowy white
That loosely flew to left and right —
The leaves upon her falling light —
Thro' the noises of the night
      She floated down to Camelot:
And as the boat-head wound along
The willowy hills and fields among,
They heard her singing her last song,
      The Lady of Shalott.

— "The Lady of Shalott"
   by Alfred, Lord Tennyson, 1842

Song of the Sparrow

I am Elaine

daughter of Barnard of Ascolat.

Motherless.

Sisterless.

I sing these words to you now,

because the point of light grows smaller,

ever smaller now,

ever more distant now.

And with this song, I pray I may

push back the tides of war and death.

So, I sing these words

that this light, this tiny

ray of light and hope may live on.

I dare not hope that I

may live on too.

I

Motherless.
Sisterless.
I am both.
But I have brothers,
    dozens
    nay, hundreds
of brothers.
Only two real ones:
brash Lavain
and my biggest brother, thoughtful Tirry.
    The others are not brothers by blood.
There are so many of them;
I call a few my friends:
    Lancelot, Arthur's second,
        but handsomer, still.
    Arthur himself, who is a captain in
        his uncle Ambrosius Aurelius's army.

The men here follow Arthur, but ultimate

fealty is to Aurelius, dux bellorum.

There is Gawain, a sweet bear of a man,

and Tristan, who is all mystery

and mischief and glee.

We live here, in this army encampment,

where drums beat and beat

in my dreams and over breakfast,

at sunrise and sundown.

The here and home I speak of

is no more than the collection of dirty,

foul-smelling tents.

I live here, in this army encampment,

among men,

because my mother is dead,

delivered into the earth

nine years ago now,

and there is no one else.

My father brought me here

when I was eight years old.

Once I heard Lavain whisper

to Tirry that it was a good
thing our mother lived to
see me through eight years
of life.
Till I was old enough to learn
to use a thread and needle
and old enough to grow
skilled at mending clothes.
At least there is
someone
left to mend their clothes,
Lavain said.
But I am just one girl,
without nearly enough hands
to sew the tears
in every man's clothing.
There are too many of them.
For, in these days,
dark battles rage on.
From all sides Britain's enemies
press in on us,

the painted Picts from the north,
marauding Scots from the west,
and the barbarian Saxons from the south
and east.
Britain bleeds
and bleeds
as men like my father and
brothers
        even Lavain
bleed and bleed.
We move as the fighting moves,
as the wind moves.
So there might be peace.

II

Before a battle begins,
the men swarm about camp
as bees in a hive, making ready.
Mount Breguoin is the eleventh fight
Arthur will lead in the war against
our Saxon enemy.
As they prepare for war, the men
ready their weapons,
sharpening blades and strengthening
shields and chain mail.
I do my part, too, tearing bandages
and brewing poultices
of healing leaves and flowers
for Cai, Arthur's steward, to carry
to the battleground.
I wander through the camp,

from the stables, which lie just near
the banks of the River Usk, toward
the center, where dirty, greyish
tents radiate out from
the great fire pit that is
the Round Table.
All the time I am
tallying in my mind the numbers
of bandages and vials of powders and balm.
The tents wind in ever-narrowing circles,
like the curves of a snail's shell.
Men huddle in groups outside
their tents, chortling with laughter at
jokes made at the enemy's expense,
rowdily singing tunes of victory.
I know them all and wave
or nod to many.
Then I spot Arthur
near the Round Table, surrounded
by a small company of men, his nearest
friends. Arthur's stance is graceful

and straight, his eyes dark as pools
in a deep wood.

There is an air of melancholy
entwined in his celebrated courage
and strength.

The men that we fight, Arthur told
me once, *they are just men. Like us.*
Well, like me, he said,
a crimson blush coloring his cheeks,
as those black eyes crinkled
at the corners with a smile.

And we fight, and ever they
come at us, like the tide
of the sea. I do not understand it.
This fighting and killing
and urge to conquer. His
gaze turned downward then.

I touched his arm, and he glanced
at me, all the sorrow on this earth
filling his eyes then.

I will never understand it.

But I will fight and kill as
I must, to protect our
world and all that is
good and just in it.
And I remember asking
myself how there could
be men like Arthur and men
like our bloodthirsty enemies,
built of the same flesh, yet so
terribly unalike.
As I approach the four men, they turn
and welcome me, grins breaking
over their faces.
Elaine! Lancelot, Arthur's
dearest friend and his fiercest
warrior calls, his emerald-green
eyes glowing.
He smiles warmly and waves me
over to join their circle.
The sight of him makes my heart
leap joyfully, and

I cannot help
but grin back at him.
Gawain is on Arthur's other side,
his friendly face shining with good cheer.
He is large and his shadow looms
over the other men, though he
is the gentlest giant I have ever seen.
Our fourth companion is
Tristan, who is not much older than I.
His golden eyes penetrate like a
wolf's, ever alert,
ever watching, but they are filled
with a mischief that never fails to
snatch a giggle from my throat.
Hello, I greet my friends.
Elaine, we were just discussing
strategies for tomorrow's battle,
Tristan informs me,
a crooked grin on his lips.
I think we should eat breakfast
before going to meet the Saxons.

We shall have to climb a mountain, after all.
We will need our strength.
But Lancelot, here, wishes to
fast in the morning, saving
himself for a celebratory lunch.
What think you? His smile widens.
I fold my hands and put my
fingers to my lips, as though I
am deep in thought.
I see I have interrupted a very serious
conversation, I reply wryly.
Yes, yes, Gawain jokes, *most serious!*
Truly, Elaine, Tristan continues
with the charade, *your knowledge is deep.*
We will do only as you command.
Ha, I crow, *if I believed that, you would*
have taken up sewing a long time ago.
The four men break into gales of
deep, rumbling laughter.
I believe our Elaine has bested you,
Tristan! Lancelot says, winking at me.

10

Come, friends, the hour grows late.
Let us to bed, for we are off at dawn,
Arthur suggests. The other three
nod their heads and we bid each other
good night.
Sleep well, and fight hard tomorrow, I tell them.
And do not forget to eat your breakfast.
I throw a smile at Lancelot as I turn to go,
their laughter following me as I make my
way back to my tent.

III

The scent of blood rides high
on the wind,
with its traces of cold, black iron,
rotted earth, dying flesh,
and I stagger backward
as the smell, pungent
and terrible,
fills my nostrils.
It stings and brings
tears to my eyes.
    I hate this rank stench.
I stand on a hill,
on a mountain called Breguoin,
beneath a young rowan tree,
its slender
grey trunk, rising
above me,

sheltering and hiding me,
protecting me.
Also a witness
to awful events.
The rowan tree's
graceful leaves and soft
white flowers
brush my arm like
a whisper. But
they do not shield me from
the stink of blood,
of death.
Men scurry beneath
me and this tree,
running hither and fro,
like ants busy at work,
but their work is the work
of nightmares.
Men in battle leathers and armor,
running hither and fro,
swords and shields raised,

and they run at each other,
hacking and slicing,
thrusting this way and that.
I watch the warring unfold,
my stomach clenched and
biting, yet I cannot look
away.
Nor can my friend,
my guardian,
the rowan tree.
Men run and fall,
sinking to their knees.
It is a dream too dreadful
to wake from.
Still, I look down, and
the grass is so green, I
cannot understand how it
does not wither and die
with sorrow. But against
an emerald carpet, the
warriors make war,

and it is like a dance,

almost beautiful,

always macabre.

The noise brings me back,

the fearsome noise of swords

striking swords,

a metallic clanging that rings in

my ears, echoing and echoing

the fearsome

din of men

screaming and crying as they

meet the sharp ends of blades.

They fall, they die.

The battle plays out like a game,

a game my brothers once played with

toy soldiers,

drums and shouts measuring

the beat.

But this war is no dance;

it is no game.

My father and brothers are down there.

My friends are down there.
In the manner of the Old Ways, I
shall sing you a song . . . I whisper
to my grey companion.
I pray to this rowan tree
to please, please keep my men safe.

I come to this place beneath the tree
to know what I, a girl,
am not supposed to know,
and never supposed to see.
So that I might know
what the men I love
endure,
that I might understand
even a little bit.
That I might have some
sense of whom and what
I will have to heal
when they return home.
    Home, the woman's domain.

But they will never keep me
at home.
I may not be allowed to fight
on the battleground,
but I share the battles
with my men
anyway.

As the clattering of swords
and shields and battle-axes
winds down, and the living
stagger from the field of
death and glory and
all that men love to
assign to fields of war,
I leave my rowan tree,
kissing her trunk, and thanking
her for keeping safe
the soldiers I love. And I
return home, ready to meet
the wounded and the well.

Ready with poultices and
ointments, bandages and
medicines.
Ready to play my part
in the fighting.

IV

Where is she? Tirry's
voice mingles with the crunch
of footsteps on frozen turf.
It is dusk now,
and I have since returned
from the bedsides of the wounded,
where I gently washed away dried
blood, where I administered tinctures
of feverfew and marigold for fever,
where I applied ointments
of calendula and willow,
poultices of yarrow and comfrey
to cuts and festering sores.
Sometimes, as I sit at the
bedside of one of the injured,
nursing a sword or arrow
wound, I cannot help but

wonder at the magic of it —
the flowers and weeds of the
moorlands and meadows
are endowed with such purpose.
Such perfect purpose.
These unassuming leaves, these
unknowing roots.
And it is for me to wield them.
Me!
Elaine of Ascolat, plain and ordinary.
But when I mix the powders
and draw out a tincture,
I feel as though some measure
of the magic has gotten in me.

Now my healing tasks are done, and
I have been waiting since
the sun finished its course,
for my father,
my brothers.

Elaine?

My father's voice,

ordinarily so gentle,

is filled with fear

and tinged with something I have not

heard in nine years.

Sorrow.

Father?

I poke my head out of the tent flap

just as Lavain pushes me aside and

charges into the tent.

He begins to light more candles,

then paces up and down the length

of the tent,

his fists and jaw clenched.

My breath catches.

Something is wrong.

Tirry and my father follow Lavain

into the tent, and

my father sits heavily on the

wooden dining bench,

his elbows leaning
on our roughly hewn table.
Each has blood,
dark brown spots, spattered
and streaked
across his face,
his hands,
his tunic.
The sight of it turns my stomach,
and I swallow back a thick,
sour taste from my mouth.
It coats my tongue.

    Strange how the blood of my

    patients does not sicken me.

Father, Tirry,
what has happened? I ask.
Elaine, my father begins, then
his voice wavers,
watery eyes betraying him.
My stomach catches in my throat,
again,

but the three men of Ascolat
are all here, safe.
Our men won the battle at Breguoin.
What could be wrong?
Please, tell me. What is it?
Tirry?
I look to my elder brother.
He returns my gaze,
Aurelius is dead.
Poisoned by a Saxon spy.
Ambrosius Aurelius,
dux bellorum,
leader of all Britons,
the general whom Arthur follows,
whom all of us follow — murdered?
As the meaning of those words
slowly becomes clear,
I hear the roar
of voices and the thudding
of boots.
Not a minute to rest from battle.

Everyone is running.
Running toward the center of camp,
to hear the news
of the death of
Britain's hope,
     our gentle leader
     our fiercest warrior.
What will happen to us?
I ask.
The Saxons, those beasts,
they will pay for this.
We will avenge this murder,
and the ground and the rivers
will run red with Saxon blood,
Lavain growls.
There is a wild look in his eye,
as if he were not now
wholly human, as if
the animal nature that lurks
in every soul,
has taken possession.

His anger fills the room,
smothers the air.
I cannot breathe.
What hope do we have left,
when the head is cut
from the body and
all the men, like Lavain,
become possessed by rage,
fear, and hatred?
When order and
faith
splinter?
Father? What will happen?
He shakes his head and
his shoulders shake.
Tirry rests a hand on Father's arm
then turns to look at me.
Hot heads, and he glances at Lavain,
will serve none of us well.
A new leader must be chosen.

As if an angel has heard us,
Arthur is coming! Arthur!
a man calls from outside the tent.
My friend's name is spoken
across the camp,
spreading like cool salve on a burn.
Arthur — he could lead us, couldn't he, Father?
I ask him, plead with him, beg him.
Please
say it is possible,
say we may be
saved.

V

My father and brothers
run from our tent and join the stomping
of boots on packed earth,
following the other
men to the center of the camp.
The warriors gather, but I am not welcome.
Or so Lavain tells me, hurling the
words like rocks over his shoulder.
Stay here. The meeting is no place for a girl.
Leaving me here, alone,
to wait and wonder.
What will become of us?
My heartbeat throbs in my ears,
like drums of war.
A quick boiling heat fills the
hole left by Lavain's callous warning.
As I watch their backs retreat,

I know I will do what I
always do.
They will not leave me here, alone.
When have I ever let them
do as much?
And so I march out
of the tent, smug and proud,
but keeping back a distance,
weaving between mud-streaked,
grass-stained tents, hovering
behind a stand of birch trees,
until I see the ring of men.
The white birch bark is silver in
the moonlight,
and the sweet perfume of leaves
mixes with the scent of living earth,
the menace of rot lurking below.

The Round Table is
Arthur's meeting hall. Beneath a
ceiling of cloud and stars,

this circle of thick, wooden benches
worn from hundreds of moons of travel and
hundreds of hands worrying their
rough, knotty surface, is placed
evenly around a great fire pit.
The Round Table is
Arthur's and his men's statement
of glory, their symbol
of brotherhood, equality.
But tonight, the brothers
grieve together.
The men circle around a bonfire,
its roaring fingers tearing into
the night.
The thrumming of sobs and
rage and violence
fills the air.
A mournful murmur is all
that reaches me.
I dare not move any closer,
and against the firelight,

the figures are darkened silhouettes.
And then I see him.
Arthur is in the center of the circle,
pacing around the fire,
hands clasped behind his back.
Then one fist cuts through the air.
My fingers find the trunk
of the tree I hide behind,
grasping its warmth,
its steadiness.
On this night when the earth
rocks beneath my feet,
the birch tree is solid.
But its
papery bark
peels away,
leaving a sticky sap
that coats my fingernails
like blood.
Arthur stands straighter than most men,
his eyes hooded and sharp.

Tirry once told me he would
follow Arthur blindfolded
and unarmed
into a battle.
I told him he'd better not try it.
But that is the power Arthur has over the men.
I wonder,
if women were allowed to fight,
would we feel the same
allegiance?
The same instincts?
Arthur is my friend, but I
cannot imagine.
Tristan asked me once if I
wished I could fight alongside
him, my family, the others.
I told him very bravely,
very boldly, *I would fight*
to protect this land,
my brothers, my father,
my friends.

Tristan laughed at this.
We hardly need protecting,
he said. *We fight to protect*
you.
I can protect
myself, I snapped back.
I know I would
fight for this country.
It is all we have,
all we are.

Now, as Arthur paces back and forth,
the murmur rises,
a gentle roar.
I rub my fingers together,
the lifeblood of the birch
sticky and hot.
There are strident voices,
and Arthur moves toward
points of the circle,

his hands moving
up
and
down,
as if he were
soothing.
Lancelot, his black hair
gleaming in the firelight,
hurries to Arthur's side,
appears to speak, then others,
Gawain, Tristan, my brothers, stand
beside the pair.
But, several men stand up
and stalk away,
away from the circle,
from Arthur's Round Table.
What is happening? I whisper
to myself.
Where are they going?
Do they leave in anger?

I hurry back to our tent,
eager for news from my brothers.
I pace the small room, the walls,
the thick folds of my
roughly woven dress
imprisoning me,
keeping me from the
affairs of men.
I live in this camp. For
more than half my life
I have lived here,
and I fight these wars
with my healing.
Why should they keep me
from the Round Table?
Again I feel my temper
begin to flare,
as happens these nights
when I am left behind.
But before this familiar frustration

can continue, Tirry and my father return.

What happened? I ask.

Arthur takes up his uncle's mantle.

He shall lead us, Tirry answers.

My father is shaking his head.

He is worn and tired.

Tirry, too, looks battered,

more so, even, than after the day's battle.

There is unrest among the men, he says.

There will be trouble.

There will be trouble.

Who will make the trouble?

Who will find it?

I do not sleep until I hear Lavain's heavy

footfalls outside the tent.

He enters and throws himself

down on his pallet, on the other

side of the sheet that hangs

between us, to give me a measure of privacy,

grunting quietly to himself.

I worry that danger will find him
before the new moon comes.
Brash Lavain.
And Tirry's words echo in my head,
There will be trouble.

VI

I remember that night,
　　nine years ago,
only in flashes,
images in my mind.
Golden leaves coated
silvery white in the
first frost of autumn.
Golden leaves on
branches gently scraping
against the thick-leaded
windows.
Father and Tirry away on
some errand, and
I asleep in my mother's bed,
warm from the fire that
was petering out,
warm from the fur covers

37

I burrowed under.
A banging on the door,
Lavain's childish voice,
high-pitched with fear.
He burst into the room,
his eyes wide with terror.
Mama! he screeched.
They are outside — they are
everywhere. Picts!
He trembled like one of those
golden leaves in the wind.
My mother moved fast.
She grabbed my arm,
her grasp so tight I gasped
with pain and surprise.
Then she took Lavain by the arm,
too, his mouth a perfect O.
He struggled,
I want to stay with you!
Then we were inside a hamper
woven of reeds,

Lavain on top of me,
and white sheets
thrown over him.
I pressed my face to the side
of the hamper,
tiny points of light
giving me a window into
the room, and my mother
standing still as stone,
a dagger clutched in her hand.
　　　She looked like a
　　　warrior goddess from the ancient legends.
I grasped Lavain's ankle or
wrist, and he was still shaking.
I watched the door, the old oak
door that had existed for hundreds of years
in this house, scarred by the touch
of my ancestors,
I watched that old oak door explode into
a thousand pieces,
a great sword, brown

with dried blood,
come through it, then an arm,
an arm painted with blue
stripes,
terrible blue stripes
followed,
and then a body painted
all over. Then two more.
Stripes and crescent
moons of blue covered their
faces and chests and
forearms.
A blue of storms and death.
    A blue to drown in.
The musty stink of the
dirty linens was too close,
stealing my breath,
and I felt my throat close.
An arm of blue moons
grabbed my mother,
forced the dagger from her hand.

It sang tunelessly as it clattered
to the stone floor.
Where are your sons? A growl,
a strange accent, a voice from
hell that stays with me
still.
I have no sons, she answered.
Barren.
barren
barren
I heard her say it.
The man who spoke first
grunted and a second
stepped forward, swords
pointed at her heart,
and I heard her gasp.
gasp
gasp
He placed his hand over her womb
then grunted to the others.
She does not lie.

does not lie
does not lie
Useless dog, the first seethed.
Then a flash and a red
rose opened up on her chest,
staining her white robe,
blooming before my
eyes.
Lavain went as stiff as a piece of wood.
I pulled my face from the tiny reed windows
and closed my eyes.
Squeezed them shut,
against the sounds of the Picts
rummaging through
my mother's chests and
drawers, picking up
her treasures and trinkets
and dropping them again.
Against the sounds of screaming
downstairs,
the voices I knew to be our servants.

Against the sound of my mother
falling to the floor.
Until we smelled smoke.
Then I was outside, the
gold leaves a mirror
of the fingers of flame
caressing the window frames,
doorways of the house,
the silver frost, an echo of smoke.
Ash fell like snowflakes,
coating our hair
eyelashes
arms
clothes.
The ashes of my home
of my mother.
We wore them for days,
as Father and Tirry carried us on
their horses, mounted before them
like sacks of grain.
Lavain did not speak.

He was silent as though those
blue devils had cut out his tongue.
I do not know for how long we rode.
I do not remember sleeping on hard turf,
or feeling cold.
Though I must have.
It was nighttime when we reached the camp.
When my mind began making sense
of what it saw and heard again.
In the torchlight I could see Lavain's face
was smeared with dirt,
streaked with ash.
His eyes were still wide with shock,
so white
so white
against his dirty ash face.
He looked like a scared, wild animal.
I must have looked the same.
Frightened animals.

Arthur, younger then,
stepped forward,
caught my father in his
arms in an embrace.
Then Tirry.
He pressed little Lavain's shoulder,
then put his hands on my hair,
petting, stroking.
And I felt safe,
a tiny bit,
for the first time again.
Poor children, he murmured.
You are welcome here,
in this camp,
into this brotherhood.
Lavain, someday, no doubt,
you will be a fierce fighter.
Aye, I can see it in your eyes.
But for now, you must take care
of your little sister.

Lavain turned away sullenly,
but I alone saw him blink
back tears.
Arthur looked to me,
What a brave girl you are,
indeed, I've never met a girl
so courageous.
There are not any others
here to keep you company,
but you have a whole army
of brothers now.
He gave a sad smile and
stepped back.
Then raven-haired Lancelot came to us,
kneeling to look in my eyes.
And I felt I was standing in
the sunlight, as though
his bright gaze alone could warm
my frozen insides.
He had blankets for Lavain and me.
And once more I felt protected.

Finally, a young boy who could not
have been more than a few years
older than Lavain
presented me with a doll
unevenly sewn of corn husks and rags.
He turned to Lavain and placed
a wooden sword in his hand.

     He said his name was Tristan.
His golden cat eyes shone in the dark,
his mouth downturned, his brow
creased as though —
as though he knew.

And it was not more than a
year later that Lancelot came for
Lavain, who still didn't speak,
still choked by rage, horror,
guilt.
Lancelot, who was the best
and bravest of Arthur's men, came
himself, for Lavain, to take him to training.

It was time for him to become
a soldier too.
I began to cry, when I saw
Lancelot's form in the entryway
to our tent.
My brother,
though silent, was my only
companion,
the only one who stayed with me
when the others left for war.
Lancelot came to kneel before me.
Why do you cry, Elaine? he asked,
brushing away a tear
with his thumb.
It was coarse, but the gesture
halted the other tears,
smoothed them away.
Because you fear you lose a playmate?
I nodded.
Well, I promise you, Lancelot told me,
if ever you feel lonely, you may

look for me, and I shall keep you company.
I stayed silent, unable to imagine
begging the famed Lancelot to
play with me.
But, true to his word,
he would come looking for me,
and he would crawl about in the dust
with me, as I prepared
banquets of berries and mud pies
for him, and he would crouch
awkwardly as we played with my doll
in the dust. As I grew older, we
ran races beside riverbanks,
and Lancelot always let me win.
Without a mother to mind me,
I ran wild, as I had seen my brothers do.
I quickly forgot the lessons in ladylike
behavior that my mother had taught me.
If I could not have her,
I would run free as a deer in the wood.
And Lancelot was my partner in freedom.

VII

I hurry to meet Lancelot in our
usual spot.
We have been in this encampment,
Caerleon-on-Usk,
for four months now.
And Lancelot and I have a
meeting spot,
next to the great elm tree
beside the horse stable.
As I race down the dirt track,
the dusty track,
that always dirties my skirt,
trying not to trip,
because I always seem to trip
when I am trying to keep my skirt clean,
I pat my hair down.
Long and not quite red or yellow,

it streams out
behind my head.
This morning I took extra care
combing my hair
with the bone comb
that Tirry carved for me,
so it would lie smooth.
I pinched my cheeks to
make them pink, but
there is so little time before
collecting and cooking the eggs
and serving my father and brothers,
to notice
if my hair is mussed
or my cheeks too pale.
These days, as I pluck the
eggs from beneath our hens, I
imagine Lancelot's smile and
wonder how grown up is
grown up enough
for him to notice I have

shaken my red-gold tresses
out of their plaits,
combed my hair
and . . . grown up?

As Lancelot approaches, he lifts
a hand in silent greeting.
He is wearing his battle leathers
and the dull winter sun
shines in his black curls.
A strange fluttering starts in my stomach.
What is this fluttering feeling?
Lately I notice how I notice
his hands
his eyes
his shoulders,
arms, and hair.
My friend.
My friend who has always
been like a brother
to me.

And now this fluttering in my belly.
These feelings are
foreign and frightening.
                    I shall ignore them.
Lancelot.
He draws to a stop and leans back
against the tree, then slides
to the ground till he is sitting.
His face is haggard
as though he has not
slept.
There is a look in his eye,
a heavy look that
makes him seem older,
as though in one night
he has lived one hundred lifetimes.
And it makes him appear
even more handsome.

Lancelot, you look . . .
Awful? he interrupts with a harsh laugh.

I nod.

Arthur is taking command.
Britain must unite behind him,
but many of the chieftains
have already deserted with their men.
Lodengrance, Loth. And there
are others.
I shall leave for Camelard in the morning,
he tells me,
to bring Lodengrance back.

I slide down beside him.

Never mind my skirts.

Why ever would British clansmen desert
Arthur now,
when he needs them most?
When we all need them?
I ask.

Lancelot shakes his head
and closes his eyes
those green eyes.
Then, blinking, he says,

Because Arthur is young. The chieftains
do not trust the young.
And the old will challenge the young
for power.
But that is ridiculous! I hear myself
whining like a small girl.
Arthur has more battle experience,
more victories than any
other clansman, soldier,
or captain.
Lancelot looks at me,
a strange light in his eye.
You do baffle me, Elaine of Ascolat.
You talk like a man; it is all too easy
at times, to forget you are not one of us.
But then the wind tugs at your hair,
pulls it loose, and I wonder
how anyone could forget that
you are, in fact, a girl.
A beautiful girl.
He catches a stray tendril of

my red hair and tucks it
behind my ear.
My breath catches.
Did he just say that?
That I am beautiful?
But a girl, he said. . . .
He does not see me
as a woman.

       Still, beautiful.

How long will you be gone?
I ask him,
feeling a heat tiptoeing
up my neck,
spreading across my cheeks.
As long as it takes to persuade
Lodengrance to give Arthur
his men and his horses.
Panic rises in my gut
at the thought of Lancelot's
absence.

Return to . . .

                    me

          us

soon, I tell him.
He nods once, then stands,
pulling me up beside him.
He takes my hand in his,
and his hands are warm and
rough like the silt and sand
on the bed of the
River Usk.
Then he brings my fingers
to his lips,
turns and walks away.

VIII

I do not think my feet have
ever carried me faster.
Not even when I was younger,
when I raced with Lancelot,
eager to show off how quick I was.
I hurry past the river,
and the sound of water
rushing over stones
slows my feet.
I stop and look at the
grassy bank, reeds
brown and green in the
springtime sunlight gently sway
with the breeze.
The scent of damp decay reaches
my nostrils, and I slip off
my leather slippers,

and step gingerly down
to the river's edge,
letting the black mud ooze
between my toes, warm
and deliciously thick.
When I wriggle my toes in
the seeping mud, a sucking
sound replies.
I remember one spring day
so many years ago now. I
was a girl of twelve,
and it was the first warm day
of spring. We were in
a different camp, beside
a different river, but it did not
look so very different from this one.
That day, the sun fell on the
grassy bank in golden pools,
dappling the boughs of a weeping
willow tree, gilding the sad,
slender leaves.

My dress hung from one of the
low-reaching branches,
waving like a
happy ghost in the warm wind,
as I bathed in the river in an undyed
woolen shift.
I kicked and paddled,
loving the feel of the icy water
on my skin, in my hair.
My brothers had taught
me to swim long ago.
Most girls did not know
how to swim.
But I could swim like
the minnows of
the stream,
and I felt so free and
the water felt so smooth,
I thought I might have
sprouted fins,
so agilely I glided through

the waters,
as the current pushed
me along.
Suddenly, a loud *plop*
and a splash came near my head.
I lost track of my strokes,
and looked up to see what had fallen.
I thought a brook trout might
have leaped into the air.
Then there was another
plop and a splash.
I looked around,
no fins, no silvery streaks
diving beneath
the surface.
And then something hard
and hot hit me in the
chest, knocking me backward.
The breath escaped from my body
in a loud puff, and I flailed
my arms, my feet kicking wildly

under the water,
searching for a slippery
rock to grasp.
Witch! a man's voice
screamed.
Witch, devil, aye, I knew
you were cursed!
I swung my head around,
looking for the voice's owner.
Then I saw Balin,
one of Arthur's knights,
Balin with his mean, hangdog
look, and cruel, hard, black eyes.
Balin! I called out, hoping that
in saying his name, he would
come to his senses and realize
that it was just me.
Not
a witch.
He wound his arm back and
launched another heavy grey

stone, this one coming
dangerously close to
my head.
Balin, stop it! I screamed again.
I am not a witch! It's me,
Elaine!
Witch, she-devil! His
voice took on a hysterical edge,
and he picked up another rock,
throwing it with all his might,
his face mottled
red and white,
twisted with fury and fear.
Balin! I could hear my own voice
tinged with desperation.
No, witch, you shall not
speak my name! You
will sink — oof!
Balin fell forward,
a look of surprise wiping away
the vicious anger.

You idiot! someone cried.

The sweet voice of an angel

filled my ears.

Lancelot, I breathed.

She — she is a witch, she is!

Look at her, she swims like

a serpent! Balin hissed

as he raised himself to his knees.

Balin, get away from here.

Lancelot's eyes filled with ferocious

sparks, and if he could have,

I am sure he would have struck

Balin down with lightning bolts

like some ancient god.

Fool! Balin spat back at Lancelot,

but he struggled to his feet,

and limped away.

Are you all right?

Lancelot's green eyes softened

in an instant.

I was treading water,

parting the current in
small swirling eddies,
as I moved my hands over the glassy
surface in circles.
Yes, I — I think so, I replied.
Thank you.
My legs felt like weights, and
my arms were shaking.
I started to swim toward
Lancelot, but the current
was pushing against
me, carrying me away,
downriver, and I hardly had
the strength to keep my head
above water.
He started to wade into the river,
but as the water rose above his knees,
he took a step back,
and slipped on one of the
slime-covered river rocks.
I could feel myself gasp

as his feet flew out from
under him and he landed on his bottom,
the water now up to his neck.
My strength was sapping away,
and I closed my eyes,
ready to be taken by the rushing waters.
Lancelot could not swim.
Then a hearty, ringing laughter
reached my ears.
I opened my eyes and saw Lancelot, sitting
in the water, his head thrown back
with mirth.
He looked at me and called out,
Hold on, Elaine! I am going to move
downriver; I will catch you!
He started to shimmy like
a crab, moving sideways,
only his head poking above
the water's surface.
With the last scrap of strength in

me, I fought against the current
and moved to close the gap between
the knight and myself.
I felt his fingers close around my wrist,
so tight it hurt,
and I allowed him to tow me toward him.
Do you think me a
witch, too, Lancelot?
I asked, my breath coming
in fits.
In that brief instant, as I
waited for his answer, I felt
myself a pink salmon,
sparkling in the sunlight,
caught in a fisherman's snare.
But when I looked up again into
Lancelot's meadow-green eyes
that smiled back at me, and
his lips made a perfect circle
as he mouthed the word *no,*

I knew I was safe.
That he would always keep me safe.

And that, I believe,
is when I first began
to love him.

IX

The shrill twittering of
a red-throated swallow
brings me back.
I slide on my shoes, ignoring
the squelching of wet mud in my toes,
and hurry home.
The brown-yellow dust
of the path
kicks up on either side of my feet.
As I reach the tent and pass
through the flaps, the stench
of animal skin turns my stomach,
reminding me
I will never grow entirely used
to living in a battle camp.
I slow myself, smoothing my
skirts. No one is in,

and I am thankful.
The scorched, scarred lid
of the old wooden trunk
    my mother's, rescued
    from the embers and ruins
    of our home
creaks open with a squeal,
and I cringe, glad
neither my father nor brothers
are nearby to hear it.
They are likely at
battle practice,
feinting and thrusting,
swordplay.
It is easy to playact with a sword,
Tirry once told me,
but the actual killing comes
much easier.
I push these awful man-thoughts
that I'm sure no other

girls entertain,

    but that plague me

    every day,

from my mind.

My mother's dresses and linens,

they will be mine when

I marry —

    though, I can't help but wonder

    if I marry — for who

    would want to marry

    a girl whose head is filled

    with man-thoughts?

The startling whiteness of her

belongings — nothing remains

white in the camp — reminds me

how little of women I know.

There it is.

A glint of metal.

I pull the silvered glass

from the trunk and prop
it on the table, against
our wooden bread bowl.
Tirry found this glass for me.
Lavain does not know I have it.
For, if he did, surely he would tease me,
call me vain and silly.
The glass is scratched, the silver
peeling away in spots.
But I can see myself
nonetheless.
Eyes of hazel-green like forest ferns
and mud,
and long, thick hair my father once told me
was the color of wheat and summer strawberries.
    Could he really think I am beautiful?
How am I supposed to tell?
I can hardly see myself as he does.
A long, skinny neck and
skin both sun- and work-worn.

My fingers move up to trace
my cheekbones, my eyebrows.
Is this what women look like?
Beautiful women?

X

My mother was beautiful.
Her face soft
and white and pink.
Her eyes the color of autumn leaves,
filled with light
and love.
I remember sitting close to her,
nose to her neck,
her scent, of
violets and earth,
warming me from the inside.
She taught me how to sew
stitches in straight lines,
gently guiding my small,
chubby hands
       small and chubby no longer,
       rather, rough and long and

callused
along the
ragged patches of
Father's torn tunics.
And I remember complaining relentlessly,
    even then,
with each stitch.
How I wished I could be
outside, playing with my brothers,
anything not to be cooped up indoors.
Now, though, I would trade all the
meadows and fields of wildflowers
for one more hour
with her.
After I had mastered sewing,
my mother sat me down before her loom.
Oh, it was beautiful, her loom.
Golden oak, polished and
smooth as her skin
but for the knots that seemed
to suggest wisdom and age.

As though the loom had seen
many lifetimes,
and knew the cares of humans,
and understood.
My mother showed me, first, how to
spin the wool, how to twist the
fibers and marry them together.
A single, continuous thread,
like her love for my brothers,
for my father,
for me,
she said,
stroking my cheek,
forgiving my complaining.
Then the weaving.
Painstakingly pulling the wool
that she had
only just spun, in and
out of itself,
back and forth,
over and over,

as patterns, stars and moons,
crosses of scarlet
and indigo emerged.

This was the safe world of women
that I knew.
No war.
No tents and no swords
or battle-axes,
no blood, no bows
and arrows,
no hordes of stinking men.
Our home was on an island,
a beautiful island in the middle of
a river, a river whose name I cannot remember.
All I can recall are the reeds along the banks
and the funny green turtles that
came to nest on the shores of our island,
        our island called Shalott.
Baby turtles,
hatching from leathery eggs.

My brothers delighted in capturing them,
building them cages of sticks,
carpeted with leaves and moss.
They would keep those turtles
as pets, as beloved as our hound, as
present in the house as motes of dust.
I remember so little of the house,
just the room in the tower,
where my mother's oaken loom
stood, where we would sit for hours,
weaving and spinning and sewing,
where golden sunlight poured in
through a single window,
painting a yellow
square on the floor.
The men of the house never entered
into that tower. It was the territory of women.
Tapestries my mother had woven
hung on the walls,
tapestries and a
singular gilded mirror.

Heavy rugs she had woven covered the floors.
But those rugs could not
suppress the damp smell of granite stones,
nor my mother's perfume of violets.
It was warm and safe there
in that tiny tower room.

Lord, I miss her.
I wish I could go back.
Back to the time when my brothers
would lead me past the weeping willow trees,
Lavain holding fast to my hand,

        when Lavain was thoughtful
        and sweet,
and they would lead me
through the rushes, down
to the banks of the river,
where they would catch those
small green turtles,

        picking them up gently,
        with such care,

where they would watch,
as warily as a pair of hawks, as I
tottered over slippery stepping-stones,
to be sure
I did not fall.

I wish I could go back to that time,
when my mother would smile
the gentle smile that told me,
all is right and well.
Back to that time when I was
young
and loved
and safe.
When we were all safe.

That things change,
that people change
        and die,
that we grow older,
that life brings the unexpected,

the unwanted,

        oh,

some days it fills me with
a measure of lightness, for
I will be a woman soon.
But other days,
the very thought
of growing older,
of not being that small girl
who danced over river rocks,
whose brothers held her hands,

            whose mother lived,

the very thought of it
crushes me,
till it is stopped,
by the world
outside
my memories.

XI

I know another woman.
She has long brown hair
that hangs about her waist.
Like me, she does not bind it up.
No, Morgan does not care for
formalities like that.
She does as she likes
and no man or woman
can say anything about it
to her.
The older sister of Arthur
is respected in her own right,
and she hears no complaints.
Morgan is the only other
female
around the camp,
but her presence is not

a constant one.

I know not where she goes.

I count days and even moons

between her visits,

the intervals seeming interminable,

as I wait for the company

of another female.

When I see her, my heart

feels free,

free to unload its

burdens,

if only

for a while.

Morgan is the only one

who knows of my fears,

the constant worries

that one day my father

or my brothers

or the three

will fail to return from battle.

And I will be all alone

in this sea of men
and war.
And she tells me,
Child, think not of those things,
those dark possibilities.
Your father and brothers are
here with you today.
Lavain will tug at your braids,
Tirry will sing you songs,
and your father will see
his wife's beauty in you.
Savor their love today.
And it will never leave you.

Morgan teaches me
her healing arts,
and I watch, rapt, as she
removes the dried herbs
so carefully from their satchels,
as she crushes and mixes and stirs.
How I love to watch

as she selects some flower
or leaf for grinding, as she explains
how a particular paste
or balm can help the skin
bind itself together, renew itself,
stave off the inflamed invasion
of infection.
It is truly amazing to witness,
and then to perform.

These powders and elixirs we brew,
they ease my worries, for I know
one less man may die or take sick
because of them.
She has given me a pouch,
a leather satchel to keep
around my neck, filled
with leaves of milfoil and
the saffron-colored petals
of calendula,
purple heads of red clover,

healing herbs
to keep close, if ever
I should need them.
She has taught me how to make
poultices and ointments,
how to chew or boil the leaves
and flowers, to plaster them
to a bruise or open cut.
To tend to the wounded.
My pouch gives me comfort.
And it also brings me a
sense of power. I
can help those I love.

Morgan's hands are white
and delicate,
but the nails are bitten
down to the quick.
Morgan hasn't the patience
for fingernails.
As I bury the mirror back

in the chest, beneath
piles of snow-white linen,
she comes to my tent, a scent of lavender
trailing behind her.
Her presence is an easy one.
Her movements are light and
smooth as a deer's.
When I am alone
I sometimes try to mimic
her fluid grace
as I set the table,
prepare the meal,
sweep the floor
of the tent.
I have noticed how Accolon,
one of Arthur's lieutenants,
watches her,
his eyes tracing

                             her motions.
If I were able to move so effortlessly,
would Lancelot watch me

in the same way?
Oh, why does my mind

                           ever wander

        back to him?
Surely he sees me
as no more than a child.
He was

    is

my friend.
Morgan is my friend too.
And after we embrace,
quickly I close the chest and
move to brew some tea.
Gently, she stops me.
Nay, Elaine. I cannot stay long.
My brother has need of me.
You see, it was my counsel and the Merlin's
that convinced him
to assume dux bellorum,
to take Aurelius's position,
to lead the Britons.

88

And I fear it does not go easily
for him now.
The Merlin is here?
My brothers did not mention him.
I have never seen him.
Some say the Merlin is a wild man, for
he lives in the Celyddon Woode,
where all manner of wild things live.
Others say he is a wise man who tells
many prophecies that come true.
Morgan says that he is a man,
both wise
and wild,
who may know the future,
and gives good counsel.
They must have spoken before
the Round Table,
for I did not see either the Merlin or Morgan
last night by the fire.
You advised Arthur? I ask
my friend, incredulously.

And he listened?
I cannot help it. I know
my brothers and father
love me. They care
for me and protect me,
but would they ever accept my counsel?
My heart sings with admiration and love
for this tiny slip of a woman
who possesses the power to move men
and the forces of a nation.
She holds to the Old Ways,
the way of the Moon Goddess,
and I sense that there
is something magical, majestic about her.

Morgan nods and looks at me
with patience and a glint of
laughter in her eyes.
And Britain will follow him,
Arthur, I mean? I ask.
Elaine, I do not know.

Her mouth twists into a
bitter grin.
But, I think most
of the soldiers will
follow Arthur. There
are rumblings, however,
and I fear more chieftains
will leave, not trusting one
as young as Arthur.
I interrupt,
What could they possibly expect
to accomplish on their own?
For it is certain that only
as a united front, could
we ever hope to defeat the
Saxons.
Yes, I know, she says,
and I swear the laughter has
returned to her eyes.
My dear, I must take my leave.
Tonight all the camp will dine together,

under the stars,
and the Merlin will proclaim
Arthur dux bellorum for all to hear.
I shall see you then.
She kisses my cheek and
goes, the tent flaps barely
rustling as she passes.
This is it, the events to be
are set in motion.

XII

As dusk approaches
and the greying light
begins to fade,
the tent flaps flap apart again.
I am sewing a tear in Tirry's cloak.
Tonight, this small task
is enough to make me feel
perfectly hopeless, there
are so many stains and holes.
Irritated with frustration, I hate
how my fingers cramp, how they
would — how I would much prefer to be
digging for roots, hunting for leaves.
As I look up, Lavain stops short.
His eyes are bloodshot, and
his flaxen hair is sticking up
in all directions, as though

he has been tugging at every strand,
trying to pull them out.
Sister. He comes near and sits
beside me on the hard wooden bench.
My hand continues to move the needle
in and out of the heavy wool.
Yes, my brother, I answer him.
These are bad days, he murmurs.
He sits silently, watching me sew.
And after a long pause, he speaks
again,
I remember Mother would sit by
the fire, listening to Tirry and
me tell her about our adventures,
her hands moving just as yours do,
guiding the needle and wool without
a thought, without
even a glance,
her eyes ever on us,
as we went on
about turtles and

snakes and minnows.

He sighs.

I wish we could

go back.

  That she would come back.

He gives a harsh chuckle.

So long ago now.

But you remind me of her,

you know.

Sometimes I forget

that you are not she.

Sometimes I forget that

I should not blame you

for leaving me.

It was her.

It was her.

His eyes close.

I am sorry, Elaine.

I am sorry.

I put the cloak aside,

and realize I have been

holding my breath.
Lavain was my dearest friend, my
closest brother
once.
But when she
died,
he
went away
too.
Became brusque,
brash, the Lavain that
I have now.
I put my hand over his
and he leans down,
down,
resting his head on my shoulder.
It is big and heavy,
and suddenly I feel small again.
We sit that way until
the sounds of my father
and Tirry approaching can be heard.

Lavain gives my hand a final squeeze
then rises.
As the others enter the tent,
he turns and reports,
Saxon troops pour into
Britain from
the southeast.
They move too near the
center of this land.
Arthur plans to attack them at
the mountain called Badon.
I look to Tirry and Father,
to see if Lavain speaks the truth.
My father nods, and looks
down, Tirry, too,
looks away.
They are ashamed,
for never have they
struck first,
on the offensive.

Come, daughter, let us
to dinner. The Round Table
is for everyone
this night.
My father takes my arm,
leans on it,
with the faintest pressure,
like an old man.
I nod my head and we
step out into the night.

XIII

My brothers walk
quickly ahead,
Lavain's strides thunderous and
harsh. Tirry's only
slightly softer.
The circle of men
is at least three deep.
An amber halo
encircles the camp,
as the flames from the
central bonfire and
surrounding smaller fires
leap and dance, shining
on the nearby tents.
My stomach begins to
feel strange, as though a
small bird has found its way

inside me,
and flies around,
frightened.
The smell of fetid yeast,
ale, and earth
fills my nostrils, and
the sparrow in my stomach
surges upward.
I swallow her back down.
Stay calm, I warn myself,
and quiet, so no one
will think to send
you back to the tent.

I spot three golden-haired
bears of men beside Arthur,
near the top of the circle.
Gawain and his younger brothers,
Gareth and Gaheris,
stand at Arthur's right side,
tall and blond, each

with a neck as thick as a
small tree trunk.
And Morgan,
her silhouette unmistakable,
in spite of loose robes,
with her long curly brown hair
flowing to her waist.
She is at Arthur's
left hand.
And there is Lancelot,
his red tunic glowing
in the firelight,
beside her.

  The sparrow quivers.
Perhaps tonight I shall talk
with him, of things that need telling. . . .

Wait.
There he is.
Against the light of the
flames,

he stands,
as though he, too,
were composed of
smoke and air.
A wraith.
But no—
Closer now, Father and I step;
he is solid and covered with flesh.
As we are.
A man.
Grey hair,
matted and wild,
falls to his shoulders.
The eyes of a predator,
an eagle,
surveying a field of mice,
or men.
I can find no kindness
in his eyes.
Two blue stripes
in the fashion of the Picts,

are painted over each cheek.
And he wears a robe
of grey twilight.
He certainly does
look like a wild man.
Could Morgan be wrong about him?

Suddenly an elbow
digs into my side.
Let us sit here, child.
My father motions
to an empty bench.
As I watch Lavain join Arthur
and his knights, I think how remarkable
it is to have watched all these men grow
from boys into men.
And now they lead.
        No, you cannot turn back time.
And now Arthur
plans to initiate an attack?
Does this make the men

murderers? I wonder.
My father and brothers
murderers?
Lancelot,
a murderer?
In the name of preservation,
we must defend ourselves,
our people, our land, is how
my father has always explained
away,
brushed aside,
my worries.
But now, his
explaining, his smoothing
away will not work.

The stink of sweat mixes
with that of ale now,
and roasting meat.
There are dozens of

men here, some I do not
recognize from our camp.
Maybe other clans, other armies
have traveled here
to witness this occasion?
I count quickly,
the men number,
it seems,
near three hundred
and sixty in all.
And two women,
myself and Morgan,
of course.
I wonder, how many
have left behind wives and
daughters, to mind the farms
and animals and land?
Not knowing whether
they live or not.
And I am so glad

not to have been
left.

I have only been
to the Round Table four
or five times before.
And then I was
too young to understand
the words and meanings.
When Ambrosius Aurelius lived,
he led small
armies of Briton men
from all over the land.
We, Arthur's followers,
were just one finger
of Aurelius's hand.
But now that Arthur
leads in Aurelius's place,
I wonder what shall
become not only of
us, but of all the armies.

Will they follow Arthur?
Or disband,
as some of Arthur's
chieftains already have?

Many men around the
circle are
so familiar.
Most of them,
as my brothers are.
Soot traces the
lines and grooves
of all these faces.
Warm spring air provides
nary a breeze.
I can feel the eyes
of some of the men
on me, tracing my shape
beneath my gown.
        Lately there is
        a change.

Does Lancelot look too?
I wonder.
Secretly, ashamedly,
I hope he does.

No, we cannot go
back.
We cannot turn back
time.

The Merlin steps forward
into the middle of the
circle, in front of Arthur.
He is like a lion.
Tirry passes a plate of
lamb to Father and me.
Britons! the Merlin shouts.
There is the rustle of
settling, then, quiet.
Britons, he repeats,
I, Taliesin, Merlin

of the Celyddon Woode,

stand before you

now, with this sword

that was forged in the fires

of Avalon, the very

beating heart

of Britain,

to proclaim Arthur,

son of the Pendragon,

dux bellorum,

defender of the land,

protector of all of Britain!

His voice booms

like thunder.

The men are rapt,

eyes wide.

Taliesin, the Merlin, is no beast —

such grace and passion form his words.

There could be no

better instrument

with which to fight,

to defend our land,
no better emblem to
stand under, to
follow, than this
sword, Excalibur,
crafted from this earth
in the sacred fires.
He thrusts the sword, point
down, into the ground, and there
is a sharp clanging sound,
as though it has struck
a rock. The sword
stands upright,
waving slightly from
the force of the Merlin's hand.
And now, Arthur, you will
draw the sword from the womb
of this land,
taking from it
that which shall
protect it.

Arthur comes to kneel
before the Merlin,
who closes his eyes
and places his hand
on Arthur's forehead,
fingers like a crown.
The Merlin's lips move,
murmuring the secret oaths
and prayers of the Old Ways.
As Arthur rises to his feet,
he wraps his palm around the
hilt of the magnificent sword,
the rubies and gold of the handle
glittering in the firelight.
Slowly, so slowly, Arthur draws
the sword forth
from the earth, and
I sense
that all the men around
me are holding their breath.
As the sword leaps

free of the soil, the
Merlin stretches out his
hands, and the men
jump to their feet as one,
and hold their own
swords aloft,
blades pointing
toward the sky.
It is as though the heavens
are thundering in answer,
the moonlight washing over
us, painting Arthur and
the Merlin in ghostly silver
light, and I swear that
there is magic at work.
A roar rises from our midst.
Arthorius, the men chant,
calling him by his Roman name,
recalling those days
of glory past,
and Arthur has

never looked so
handsome or strong.
His fingers are pocked
by tiny white scars
I imagine he received in battle.
Fight with me,
beside me,
under the sword
Excalibur.
For Britain, he roars.
For Britain, everyone
echoes.
And my voice joins those of the men.

XIV

I watch as Tristan unslings
his harp from its place on
his shoulder.
The frame is delicately carved
of sleek grey ash wood,
and it shines and sings, the music of the
strings ringing long after they have
been struck.
Tristan runs his fingers
over the strings, raising a
melody that reminds me
of a brook that trickles and
glides across the landscape,
clear and musical, careless
and free.
He sings of battles and
ancient warriors,

victories over dark enemies,
and sunshine and glory.
His voice is also like water,
smooth and warm,
fluidly tripping
over notes and words.
He calms the men into
a relaxed state of delight.
They clap their hands
and sing along,
but no matter how loudly
they sing, no one can
match or conceal
Tristan's rich, lilting voice.
I turn to look upon the faces that I love.
Gawain and his brothers,
my father, my brothers — even Lavain looks
cheerful and at peace, this once.
A light seems to radiate from within
all of them, as though
a fire has been lit inside their

very souls.

And there, there is Lancelot,

knight of my heart.

He who has been

playmate and friend,

guardian and protector.

I love him.

I love him.

I do.

Should I tell him?

Tonight under this moon . . .

Before he rides away . . .

Slowly, the men begin to rise

from their seats,

draining the last dregs

of their ale, and find their way

back to their tents,

content and ready to rest.

As my father and Tirry bid me good

night, and Lavain finds a place

with a group of men who are still

carousing and laughing loudly,
I stand and move closer to Lancelot.
His green eyes light up, and he
nods as he sees me approach.
I find a seat by his side and
wait for the end of the song.
Good evening to you, Elaine.
Lancelot turns to me and smiles.

   The sparrow leaps.
Hello, I manage to whisper,
sending a silent prayer of thanks to the
Moon Goddess for the cover
of darkness that hides the warm blush
crawling up my neck,
coloring it crimson.
*You look lovely by the light
of the fire,* Lancelot says,
looking at me lazily.
He turns in his seat to study me.
He must be able to hear
my heart beat.

I curse myself for not combing
my hair again, for not
brushing the day's dust and dirt
from the hem of my dress.
But the coarse yellow wool
glows golden in the firelight,
and under his heavy gaze,
I can almost imagine it is a proper
gown.
It is funny, he murmurs
thoughtfully, *it was just today that
I told you we could not help
but forget sometimes
that you are a girl. Yet,
tonight I saw how the men look
upon you. You are grown up now,
Elaine. A woman.*
His fingers flutter at the nape
of my neck.
My heart flutters too.
He called me a woman.

He believes I am a woman!
And the thought of his watching me,
it sends such delicious sensations
up and down my spine.
Aye, he continues, *a woman does not*
belong to this hard battle-camp life.
His hand has moved to rest on mine,
his fingers so lean and strong.

                    The sparrow beats her wings.

Hard times draw near,
Lancelot murmurs.
Yes. I find my free fingers toying
with the leather satchel
around my neck.
Tell me, Elaine,
does this amulet make you
feel safer? Lancelot asks,
reaching to pull the
pouch from my hand.
It is no amulet, I tell him.
I wear it so I always have

herbs for healing close at hand,
in case you find trouble,
as you always seem to do.
My teasing is flat, and a shiver
grips me.
I have no business joking
about such things.
It can only tempt ill fortune.
Lancelot sighs, his eyes downcast
and weary.
I wish the day would arrive
when you no longer need
to wear such a necklace.
I would bring you a necklace
of the most beautiful
pearls from the distant seas.
He looks up at me, his laughing green eyes
boring into my own.
Now my little sparrow
threatens to break free, fly away.
You would? I ask breathlessly.

Aye. Lancelot looks at the fire
then turns back slowly and
grins at me. *I would bring you
all manner of pretty trinkets.*
I love presents, I reply,
breathless.
What else would you bring me?
Lancelot's smile widens.
I would find you the most beautiful . . .
He rolls his eyes around,
as though searching for the
right answer, then stops,
looking up at the night sky.
He points at the heavens.
. . . the most beautiful star in the sky.
See there, that one.
He leans close to me, and I breathe
in his rich, musky scent.
My heartbeat quickens.

    Now?
    Do I tell him now?

Alas, Lancelot groans, moving back,
we are here in this camp,
about to march off to war,
and I have a duty to perform in the morning.
And so I will bid you farewell.
I shall see you upon my return
from the summer lands.
My stomach sinks. I had forgotten
he was leaving for Camelard.
Safe journey, Lancelot.
I will wait for you to return.
He smiles again and bows his
head ever so slightly, then
with his marked grace,
rises and leaves.

As I watch him move away,
I can hardly quell the twitches
of nervous excitement in my belly.
Could it be?
Does he

love me?

I sit back on the bench as the
fire begins to fade and die out.
Then suddenly someone is beside me.
Lancelot?

Tristan. I start with surprise.

Your singing was beautiful tonight,
I tell my friend.

*Why, thank you. I am
pleased to hear it,* he says.

*There is no other
who can ease our hearts
as you can with your music,*
I say.

You flatter me. A gleeful
smirk crosses his mouth, before
a crooked half-smile that is all too
contagious steals its place.

*Really, Tristan, you have a way
of making everything feel right
and well.*

He lays the harp gently on the
ground.
Well, as long as you think so,

and the others, too,

that is all that matters.
His cat eyes glint in the firelight.
I pour a cup of mead for him and
one for myself.
He drinks long and thirstily.
How do you always know what
we need, before we know ourselves, even?
he asks. His eyes
no longer teasing.
What do you mean? I feel a
pink heat returning to my neck,
reaching for the tips of my ears.
You were singing. I thought
you might be thirsty, I tell him.
I was.
He nods, but his eyes
are thoughtful.

Tristan's face is sober.
He scuffs his toe over a clump
of clover.
Singing is fine and easy
on a night such as this one,
but I would that this warring
would end, he says.
It has lasted too long,
and too long we have not made
time for normal life.
We have stood up and
are walking now, away
from the firelight, toward
the copse of birch trees.
The moon plays
on the ground in pools of
ghostly light.
As we walk between the trees,
their bark peels away
from the trunks
like scrolls of silver parchment.

What would such a life
look like? I ask.
It would look as life should,
husbands and wives living
in quiet homes, with
children playing in gardens,
without fear of Saxon invaders
carrying them off.
You could marry your knight —
he breaks off and looks at me
devilishly for a moment.
My knight? I ask, my heart
beating faster.
I know you too well, Elaine, he says.
I do not know what you are talking about.
I circle the nearest tree, my head spinning.
How has Tristan guessed?
Do all of the men know?

     Does Lancelot know?
Oh, come, Elaine, I see how you
gaze on him, upon Lancelot.

Don't be ridiculous, Tristan, I retort.

All right. He is grinning again.

Perhaps I am ridiculous.

Perhaps I deserve this life

of violence. But, truly,

I would live a life of peace,

free of ill-fated, ill-brought . . .

Tristan's voice trails off.

What? What is it? I ask him,

circling back around to where

he stands.

Elaine, do you know how I arrived

here, under Arthur's watch?

I had always assumed that he came

to be here as so many others did,

having lost family and home to

marauders.

I was sent here by my uncle.

Sent? I ask.

Tristan takes a deep breath,

then pushes on.

My parents were both killed, and
so I went to live with my uncle
Mark, but after,
after his wife, Isolde —
His voice breaks off, his lips
still bent around the shape
of her name,
as though he savors it, keeping it close.
After Isolde began to look
on me in a way unbefitting of
an aunt, he sent me away.
Suddenly those eyes that are
usually filled with so much
light and laughter turn dark,
filled up with sorrow.
I feel my own eyes grow wide with surprise.
We have never spoken so seriously,
nor at such length.
And I admit, he continues, *I was not*
entirely innocent, either.
But you must have been a child!

I exclaim.

Yes, and so was she.

She was too young to be wedded

to an old man, and her mother,

knowing this, cursed us both.

But why? I ask. *Why you?*

None of this makes sense.

She gave Isolde a potion,

a draught to drink

to make her love my uncle.

But, mistakenly, I drank of it, too, and was

thus cursed. We deceived my uncle,

and when he learned of it,

he banished me from his kingdom.

Tristan looks up at me, his

eyes piercing the farthest

reaches of my soul.

And so you see, love holds no

promise for me. I shall never love

again. He looks away.

And thus, this life of

war is the one for me.
Tristan, I say shakily, *it was*
not your fault. Do not say such things.
I want to pull him
from this black mood, from these
blacker thoughts.
He chuckles grimly.
Now you know my dark secret.
It was long ago, and while I
cannot forgive myself, distance
has been kind. And every day
I feel grateful
that the betrayal was not requited.
He looks thoughtful,
far away, but then he comes back
to me.
Well, I am not sure how
it is that I came to tell you all this,
but let us talk of happier things.
Yes, I say, *let us wish for days*
of peace, when we may make our

home in a copse of birch trees,
like this one, without fear,
without cursed love.
He stares at me curiously.
Then says, *The hour grows late.*
I must get you back to your father.
In the moonlight, I could swear
that Tristan is blushing.
But we bid good night to the
silvery trees and bid good night
to each other outside my father's tent.

XV

The camp feels different this morning.
It is as if the sunlight has
swept clean the
muck of fear and uncertainty.
The air smells fresh and
is filled with . . .
hope?
Even the horses
seem to feel it.
As I pass the stables,
I can hear the stamping of
hooves, restless snorting, and
excited whinnying.

I am down by the
River Usk, washing out
laundry, pounding

sheet against stone, rubbing
sand into the folds, rinsing
and scrubbing and
wringing.
On most days, I would hate this
dull, backaching chore,
but on this brilliant morning,
the scent of soap and lard
lingers in the spring air,
mixing with the perfume
of daisies and all that is
living in this world.
            And it does not bother me
one whit.
The rich melody of
the blackbird's flutelike call
beckons to me,
and then I hear
the rumble of footsteps
and voices.
There she is!

a booming
voice calls out.
A golden-haired head
is now visible over
the crest of the hill. Then,
another, and a single, darker head.
Gawain, his
youngest brother, Gareth, and
Tristan
are coming my way.
Elaine, what are you doing?
Tristan's voice is cheerful and,
as he moves ahead of
his companions and nears, his
yellow-green cat eyes
glow with mirth.
What does it look like
I am doing? I retort,
smiling back at him.
How can you do laundry
at a time like this?

He grins and Gawain and
Gareth lope down the bank
and come to examine
my basket of linens.
The day is a beautiful one,
a day of new beginnings.
It is not a laundry day, Tristan scolds.
We are off to fight by the
rise of the new moon,
Gareth adds eagerly,
clapping his brother
heartily on the shoulder.
He is like a small boy
boasting of a new toy.
And Lancelot shall return
by tomorrow, noon,
Gawain intones.
Tristan stretches like a cat.
The men joke
that he is by far
the most handsome of them.

But I prefer Lancelot's
dark looks.

                              What?

I never used to have these
thoughts.
What has come over me?
But the mention of Lancelot's name
quickens my heartbeat, though I
try not to let my feelings show.
Tristan studies me closely, and when
our eyes meet, I drop mine abashedly.
He grins.
Nothing escapes his notice.
I twist my hair into
a knot at my neck,
realizing how improper
I must look,
mud on my knees, my
skirts tied around my thighs.
Quickly, I unloose my dress,
and glance up to see a red blush

creeping over three
unshaven faces
at once.
Come, Elaine. Tristan
is the first to break
this awkward silence.
Come and eat with us.
All this washing must be making
you hungry, and you should
not delay your noontime meal,
for there is to be
another feast tonight by
the Round Table.

I try to recall what
was life like
before these boys,
these men.
And I wonder, what
would life have been like
if I had never known them,

if Mother had lived.
Surely I would miss them.

I wring the moisture from the last sheet
and fold it quickly, laying it
on top of the rest of the laundry.
I will hang everything to dry after lunch.
As we walk back to the center of camp,
Gawain keeps pace with me, matching his
longer stride to my
shorter, quicker one.
You are looking forward to
the fighting? I ask the
great giant of a man,
looking up into his friendly
face that is ruddy with sun.
Tiny lines crisscross
at the edges of his eyes.
The fighting ages him, too.
I do not think it fair
to say I look forward

to it, Gawain replies.
Gareth is young and
still eager to prove his worth
in battle. But, as you must know,
our father, Loth, is one of those chieftains
who left two nights ago. I
cannot help but feel as
though I must fight harder,
must prove myself all over again
to make up for my father's absence.
It is unforgivable, his leaving.
And I am ashamed.
Gawain looks down.
But Arthur surely knows that
a father's acts say nothing
about his son's, I say. *Your mettle*
and worth have been proven
time and again, Gawain. There
is not a man in this camp who
believes you are in any
way responsible for Loth's

leaving.

What about woman? he
asks with a rueful grin.
Nor woman, I tell him,
patting his huge hand.
*Elaine, you are a true
friend,* he says.
I can detect a trace
of gratitude in his voice,
as though a fear has been
allayed.
And we walk on, through
the camp, together, in silence.

XVI

By the rise of the new moon.
Gareth's words echo over
and over in my mind.
The moon begins to wane.
This means the men will leave
within a fortnight.
How many times have I
watched my father,
Tirry, and Lavain march off
to fight? More than I
can count.
But this feels different,
final, somehow.
A seed of dread
has begun to flower in
my belly, and tears spring and
sting my eyes.

How will I ever let them go?
The nearness of their departure
has brought me back to
sewing, odious chore it is.
But I must finish mending
Tirry's cloak before he leaves.
Before he leaves.
Suddenly a sharp pain
shoots through my
finger.
Droplets of blood leak
onto the heavy wool
of the cloak.
I've pricked myself,
something I haven't done
in years.
I watch the blood spread,
swallowed by
strands of thread,
sinking, darkening, staining.

      An omen?

I feel my throat closing, thick
with tears, and I cannot breathe.
I drop Tirry's cloak to the ground,
throwing it from my lap
as if it itself is a curse.
Then I run from the tent,
tears blinding me.
My feet lead me to the
birch trees.
I stumble to the
ground.
The earth is soft and cool,
carpeted with leaves here.
I lie down, my cheek against spongy moss.
Teardrops slip off my cheeks,
making small wet pools on the ground,
on my hands. They slide into my mouth,
the salty taste
stinging my tongue.
The tears come faster,
burning my eyes.

I cannot stop crying,
afraid that I have courted
disaster, horrible images
of brothers, father, friends
in pain, running through my mind.
This battle, Arthur's plan —
I am so frightened of it.
Then I hear the whisper of
footfalls approaching.
I look up to see Morgan,
wrapped in a robe of indigo,
standing above me.
Elaine! Worry seeps from her voice.
What is wrong? What is it?
B — b — *bad omens.* But I am crying
too hard to explain.
My dear, hush, Morgan
kneels beside me and
strokes my hair.
Panic and fear fight
to consume me.

Warm arms so thin
they feel like a tiny robin's
wings encircle me.
I lean into Morgan's embrace,
allowing her to continue petting my head.
Morgan, I whisper,
I am sorry.
Hush, child. Be still.
No apologies.
Her breath is soft on
my cheek,
mixing with hot tears.
I spread open my hands and a faint
dot of dried blood marks
my finger.
What is it, Elaine? What
has upset you so?
I am so frightened, I tell her.
Frightened, dearest?
Morgan continues to stroke
my hair as though I were a small child,

as my mother did when I tripped
and scraped my knee or
knotted my wool as we were weaving.
What are you frightened of? Morgan asks.
Losing them, my father. My brothers, I reply.
This march on the Saxons, I continue,
it does not feel right. And now,
now I have gone and given
Tirry bad luck.
How did you do that? Morgan murmurs.
I — I pricked my finger as I was
mending his cloak. And I
left a spot of blood.
The blood — it is an omen.
I am afraid to let them go.
The tears return, filling
my eyes, spilling down
my cheeks.
I wipe them away as quickly
as they fall.
Shhh, Elaine, come with me, Morgan says.

Let's get you washed and calmed.
And we can talk
of these things.
She helps me to my feet
and leads me back to her tent.
It is on the other side
of the camp,
nearer to Arthur's.
Once I am seated in the cool interior,
she puts a cup of wine
in my hands.
I take a sip, its
sour heat warming my throat,
clearing away the bitter taste of fear.
She brushes a damp cloth
scented with lavender
over my forehead,
down my cheeks and again,
I think of my mother's calm hands
easing my childhood terrors.
Let us talk, Morgan says.

I nod and draw a deep breath.

This march on the Saxons,

I understand it, but

it scares me, I explain.

Our men have always defended this

land, its villages and people,

as the Saxons or Picts have

attacked.

But they have never met our

enemies in a battle of our own

making.

Morgan looks thoughtful, then says,

Yes, it is true. Her brow wrinkles as

she considers her words.

But I cannot help but feel

this battle, too, is of the Saxons' making.

A tall shadow suddenly fills

the tent entrance.

Brother. Morgan looks up

as Arthur haltingly enters.

My sister. Arthur gives

a small bow. *And Elaine.*

He looks surprised as he notices

me. *Am I interrupting?*

He looks unsure.

His eyes flick from

                              Morgan's face

to mine.

Oh, Arthur, enter. Morgan sounds

almost

impatient with her younger brother.

Certainly I interrupt.

Arthur smiles uneasily.

May I help?

Morgan glances at me,

a question in her eyes.

It is my choice,

to include Arthur or not.

I have known him so

many years now, and he has

long been a friend.

But today he is different.

Today he is dux bellorum.
I shift in my seat,
suddenly nervous.
Arthur, I begin.
I am about to tell the leader
of all Britons that I
disagree with his strategy.
What am I thinking?
What right do I have?
Yes, Elaine? Please, what is it?
I can see something troubles you,
he says.
I must admit, I begin, my voice
trembling, *I am frightened.*
For the first time, I think, Arthur laughs
gently, *our brave Elaine admits*
fear? I do not believe it.
He grows serious. *Please, Elaine,*
tell me what troubles you.
I take a deep, shaky breath.
I am frightened by the plan

to attack the Saxons.
Initiating a battle seems,
somehow —

      I search for the right words.

wrong.
Murderous.
Most of all, I — I fear
it will only invite ill fate.

Arthur sits slowly on the bench
nearest me. His
eyebrows are knit together,
and he appears to actually
be weighing my words.
We have shared jokes and
casual words so often.
But talk of battle plans?
Never.

Elaine, I would be lying
if I said I had not considered
these same arguments carefully.
We have always fought

defensively, waiting till our villages
were attacked. The thought of our
meeting the Saxons offensively
sickens me. That we have to
meet them at all saddens me.
But they continue to pour into
our land, unhindered and in
great numbers.
We must meet them and
stop them,
drive them from our shores
for good.
Now.
I fear that if we wait
any longer, we will not be able to
stop them. They will outnumber us,
and they will have reached too far into
the heart of this land. I fear they will
stamp out the Britons, enslaving us
and bending us to their will. They
are so many, and we are so few.

So very few.

He looks as though a very
heavy load rests
on his shoulders.
Indeed, I imagine,
that load is real.

Arthur — I begin.

No, do not apologize
for declaring your fears,
he says.

I would there was another way.

But I cannot see one.

He pauses.

Elaine, I remember the first time
I met you.

You were so young,
so scared. It nearly broke
my heart to see you so.

I look up at him, tears in my eyes.

Morgan sits beside me and squeezes my hand.

Those were bad days, I whisper.

Yes, Arthur intones.
But these are better days, for
my heart is filled with much gladness
to see how strong you are.
And I am grateful, Arthur continues,
for your skills in the healing arts.
You have saved more than
one life. And I am grateful for
your friendship. We are
all grateful for it.
Arthur looks straight at me.
He stops again and clears his throat.
I wonder, may I speak openly with you?
Of course, Arthur, I reply,
my curiosity growing.
Do you know, he begins uncertainly,
how I came to be dux bellorum? he asks.
I am not sure I understand.
You are the nephew of Aurelius — I begin.
The Merlin, the Merlin and my sister
came to me — *before Aurelius was killed,*

154

and they foretold his death.
My eyes widen, and I look at
Morgan. She nods, her
lips pursed tightly. Arthur laughs
grimly. *I did not believe them.*
They spoke the truth, and
I did not warn Aurelius! he moans dolefully.
I had the knowledge, and
I did not use it to save him.
Again, I look to Morgan, who
just shakes her head and looks away.
She rises and begins to pace
around the tent, her steps stormy.
Arthur, I know not of these things,
the magic of the Merlin, I tell him,
but you did no wrong.
His eyes are wild, and he continues,
his voice ragged. *That is not all.*
The Merlin told me it was all part of a
prophecy. I would take Aurelius's place
as dux bellorum, and I would lead

155

the Britons to victory. He gives another
harsh laugh. *I — who am I? How
can I ever lead all these men?
What if I lead them to their deaths?
And all of this weighs on me, ever
plaguing my sleep, my dreams.
But I have no choice.* His face
is pale and his lips set
in a thin, bloodless line.
No choice, he repeats. *I would
that things were different.*

My mind whirls as I try to think
what to say to him.
There are no words to comfort him,
so great are his worries.
What a burden, what a weight,
I think. How unfair.
Arthur, I start, unsure of
how to continue. *I believe in you.
The men believe in you. There
is no one else whom the men*

will unite behind. They love you.
And though these burdens
sit heavy on your shoulders in the
face of such dark deeds to come,
I have faith that all will be well.
That you will be well. And as
I speak the words, I realize that I
truly believe them. And from
the look of relief that lightens his brow,
I can see that Arthur does too.
Morgan is staring at us both and
comes to stand beside Arthur,
resting her hand on his shoulder.
Elaine speaks wisely, she murmurs.
Yes, Arthur replies. *She says much the*
same as you do, Sister.
Thank you, Elaine, he says,
turning to me. *I am sorry*
to have passed my worries
onto your shoulders, but to have a
friend, an ear — for that I thank you.

Arthur rises and bows, then
turns to Morgan, lifting her
hand and pressing
a gentle kiss to it.
Then he turns to leave,
throwing a last, small smile to us.

Slowly, I step out into the
cool evening air.
My feet,
my legs feel as light as
a cat's.
I pad slowly back to the great
elm tree where Lancelot
and I meet, the elm tree
made grey by the moon's light.
I sink to my knees, and lean
back against the
unyielding trunk, grateful
for its solidity, its weight, and
its rough, scratchy bark.

I am glad that
it is for me to see
the side of Arthur,
of the men I love,
that they dare not
show each other.

I must do something.

XVII

As I wander distractedly back to
our tent, thinking about how
the warring steals choices from all of us,
I hear footsteps
behind me. Quickly,
I turn, forgetting momentarily
that Lancelot has left.
Tristan. I hope he does not
recognize the disappointment
in my voice.
Yes, it is I, he laughs.
*It is late for you to be
out, no?* he asks,
his eyebrows raised in question.
Yes, I suppose it is, I answer.
Late, that is.

Muddled.

What is it, Elaine? You sound strange.

It is —— it is nothing, I tell him,

shaking my head to clear it.

Nothing? he murmurs.

I was just —— just thinking about

the herbs I must collect before

you leave.

I see, he says, not sounding like

he could see at all.

You are not plotting anything,

are you? he asks, his eyes glowing

in the gathering dark.

I know of your inclination to follow

where you should not.

I stop, surprised, no longer

distracted in the least.

What? I ask.

You heard me, he says,

his hand touching my

elbow.

I know of your secret visits
to the Round Table,
to battlefields.
You must not try to follow us,
Elaine.

I — I had not thought to try.
But as I speak the words,
a tiny voice begins to
whisper in my mind.

Promise me, he commands, urgently.

I promise, Tristan.
But I know now that I lie.

Very well, he says.
Though I hardly trust you.

He is grinning again,
his leonine eyes dancing.
Tristan delivers me to the mouth
of my tent, and I bid him a
good night.

And as I lay down on my pallet,
a plan starts to take shape.
There is much work to be done.
Thank you, Tristan, I whisper.

XVIII

Morning dawns grey
and ominous, the sky
pregnant with indigo clouds.
As I rise from my bed,
I sense that I am alone
in the tent, my family
already gone to the mock
battlefield. In these
moments of silence
I do my chores, sort through
my herbs and take stock of
what is needed.
Handling the colorful powders
and scented flowers calms me,
allows quiet into my head.
I must think on my plan.
A list begins to form in my mind,

and suddenly I wonder, how will
I ever manage to gather all that
I might need and prepare
a kit for the journey
without anyone seeing, guessing?
For I shall follow.
There are no hiding places in this
tent, no private spots
in this camp.
As I scan the room, looking
for a nook to secret away
a sack, my eyes fall
upon my mother's chest.
Yes, there should be room inside
of it, to squirrel away medicinal
plants, some clothes and food.
And no one will think to look in there.
The domain of woman.

I hear a scratching outside the tent,
and then Tristan's voice floats

in to me, *Your knight returns,*
Elaine. Will you come to greet him?
　　　　Chastise him or cheer?
My heart does a little
flutter and I long to run outside,
but for Tristan's sake, well,
for my own sake, that I might be
spared further teasing, I slow my feet.
I am sweeping, Tristan. And I do
not know the man whom you call
'my knight.'
Is it my father?
I had no word
that he has left.
I smile a secret smile, then
step outside to meet my friend.
Shall we? Tristan asks, grinning as
he escorts me to the far edge of the camp
that overlooks the great moor to the west.
See there, he points, and I can just
make out tiny smudges riding

on the horizon, far off in the distance.
There is Lancelot with a small party.
It looks as though he succeeded
in the task Arthur set for him.
The hazy figures soon resolve into
solid shapes and indeed I can
make out several horsemen
and a carriage.
Does Lodengrance ride in the coach?
I ask. *Can he not ride with the other men?*
I know not, Tristan replies, thoughtfully
stroking his chin.

Soon I can discern Lancelot riding
at the fore on his beloved white stallion.
A heavyset man rides beside him.
Lodengrance.
So, who, I wonder, rides in the carriage?

A rustling behind me draws my
attention, and I see Arthur approach.

He nods and comes to stand beside me.
I look at him, but am met only
with his profile, as he
studies the nearing company.
His presence is unquiet,
and now Tristan, too, shifts
restlessly beside me.
My feet long to run away,
but my heart stays them.
My heart, like a baby bird,
longing to see Lancelot, jumps and
dips in anticipation of our reunion.
Finally the riders are here.
Lancelot dismounts
his steed without even a glance
my way.
He moves directly to the carriage,
with a look on his face such as
I have never seen there before,
so intent and serious it is.
But there is something else

in his green eyes,
something I do not recognize.
The carriage door is thrust
open, and I feel my companions
draw a collective breath,
as we wait to see who
alights.

Then,
the most beautiful creature
I have ever seen emerges.
She has a crown of hair the color
of flaxseed, skin ivory and delicate,
and full coral lips.
Her gown looks as though
it is woven of silver gossamer,
spun by enchanted spiders
for a faerie princess.

A girl!
A friend?

A companion to teach me all that
I do not know of women and beauty
and fine manners?
A friend to share my secrets and wishes?
Who will tell me her own?
          A friend?
Lancelot takes her hand and
assists her to the ground.
And he looks stricken,
as though some force
grips his heart or his stomach,
or both.
The girl's seashell lips lift
into a gentle smile as she
places one dainty hand on
Lancelot's arm, allowing
him to escort her to
where we stand.
Lancelot has not taken his
eyes from her face.
Indeed, he looks enthralled.

Arthur looks down fleetingly
and draws a breath,
as though steeling himself,
then steps forward to meet them.
My friends, he says, his hands
extended before him in greeting.
To my surprise, Lancelot,
who has been Arthur's dearest companion
for as long as I have known the pair,
does not turn to his captain.
Rather, he continues to stare in
an almost unnatural manner
at the young woman who stands by his side.
Lodengrance, who is as ruddy-faced and
rotund as I remembered him, approaches
Arthur first, throwing his arms open and
embracing him.
Ah, my dear friend. It gives me great
pleasure to be back in your company.
Soon I shall call you 'Son,' eh?
Lancelot flinches.

What is happening here?
The way Lancelot gapes
at this strange girl is
unnerving, and a dull ache
opens up in my chest.
It feels as though there is a
yawning hole where my heart
did beat hopefully
just some minutes ago.

I do not understand what unfolds.
And the girl, she stands there,
so placid, gazing on Lancelot,
then turning to Arthur,
who now returns Lodengrance's
embrace, and says,
You are most welcome here.
Indeed, I thank you for coming
and bringing some measure
of cavalry to our aid.
We have great need, in these

days, of friends. I am
happy to see you, old friend.
I cannot stand here, I cannot
watch this tableau,
which I do not understand

                    nor do I want to understand it,

unfold any longer.
But I cannot look away.
Nor can I stop the torrent
of questions.

XIX

Finally the greeting party
breaks apart.
Tristan returns to his
weapons practice,
and Arthur leads Lodengrance
and the girl away.
Lancelot stands rooted
to the spot, as though frozen.

I hurry back into my tent to
find some mending, something
to keep me busy, so the
doubts filling my gut do
not carry me away.
Then I cannot stand it
any longer, and the walls
of the tent seem too close,

too stifling. I must get
outside.
As I run to the willow
tree at the river's edge,
gulping great breaths
of sweet fresh air,
I stop short. There
is the girl, and she is
with Lancelot. His arms
are around her, and she
lifts a hand to his
cheek. He is murmuring softly
to her. I cannot trespass;
I cannot believe what I see.
The ground feels as though
it bends and shifts beneath me.
Indeed, the world feels as though
it rocks in its place in the heavens.
Will we all fall down?
The pair stand partially hidden
by the willow's low-sweeping branches,

and my stomach
turns and churns.

    Lancelot, with the faerie girl.
This is all so wrong!
I know not what to do.
I cannot bear to face anyone
now.
I circle around the perimeter and
finally find the great elm by the stables.
I sink to the ground. My breath
comes unevenly
and my head spins.
What has taken hold of Lancelot?
What spell has this yellow-haired
sorceress cast on him?
I look at my hands,
freckled with sun,
callused from so many chores.
The nails are ragged and
torn; dirt lodges

beneath them in grey crescents.
Her hands, her hands are so
white, with long tapering fingers
with smooth, rounded nails.
The essence of woman.
All the memories of my
mother's face, all the ideals
of what a woman should be,
they are all wrapped up
in her.
And I am so dull and dirty.
Like a small brown toad.
He does not see me.
How could he see me
when she is before him?
Glowing and gilded in gold.

Then Tristan is before me,
his face a stiff mask.
Elaine? His voice is hesitant.

I cannot respond, I cannot
summon my voice.
O, and tears threaten.
I look at the moss and
the grey pebbles and
withered leaves around
my feet.
He is beside me.
His hand covers mine.
Elaine, Tristan repeats.
Are you — are you well?
I am not sure how to answer him.
I am not sure *if* I am able to answer him.
I rub my fingers over the thick,
springy moss.
His hand tightens over mine.
What — what happened? I
manage, croaking
like a bullfrog.
Tristan leans his head back

against the trunk and sighs,
moving his hand into his lap.
I am not certain if I understand
it, he murmurs.
I believe Lancelot lured
old Lodengrance back here
with the promise of Arthur's hand.
Arthur is a man of means, and
I suppose he shall marry
Gwynivere, daughter of Lodengrance.
Arthur to marry this girl?
All of the words Arthur spoke
that night in Morgan's tent
skip through my memory.

> *I would that things*
> *were different . . .*

. . . that things were different . . .
It makes sense now.
Now I understand.
He must have known.

All these machinations,
and I so naive.
Lancelot looks bewitched, I spit,
surprised by the vitriol in my voice.
Yes, he does. Tristan looks
at me appraisingly, his eyes
darker now beneath eyebrows
raised in question.
Love is a tempestuous mistress,
he continues. *And none of us*
shall ever master her.
He rises to his feet,
his eyes slanting as he looks
down on me,
Do not fear, Elaine,
love and friendship will
resolve themselves.
I continue to rest below
the elm tree, the moss
and leaves and bark,
solid and familiar,

like an anchor.
I want to believe Tristan,
but I do not see a way for
anything to be all right
again.

XX

What place does a woman
have here, in this
realm of men?
I wonder.
　　　But I do have a place.
I belong here, with these men.
They are my family.
I mend their clothes,
I mend their bodies.
I grew up wild like a boy
here.
How could *she* possibly belong here,
to this camp?
Her clothes are far too
clean for these dusty soldiers,
dusty tents.
Yet, I always dreamed of a girl

coming to live here, of a girl
who would be my friend.
Elaine. A deep voice interrupts
the torrent of self-pitying thoughts.
Tirry is towering over me,
Why have you been hiding here?
he asks. *Did you not hear*
that there is a girl come to camp?
I shake my head, unable to answer.
You have been summoned to the
Round Table, he explains.
Who summons me? I ask crossly.
Arthur, Tirry answers.
He wishes you to come and
meet his future bride and
let her know that she is not
alone here.
Of course she is not alone
here, I retort. *There are*
nearly three hundred and fifty
men dwelling here in this camp.

I do not know why you are
angry with me, Tirry says,
looking wounded.
I am not angry with you,
Tirry. I will come. I know
my voice sounds resigned.
I am resigned.
I follow my brother back
to the center of camp,
my feet dragging, stirring
up more dust, which settles
on the hem of my gown.
The nubby wool, once vermilion,
is now brown from wear and dirt
that no amount of washing can remove.
My slippers, doe-brown leather,
too, are covered in a fine layer of
grime. Nothing, nothing about me
is fine.
When we reach the fire pit
where the Round Table meets,

the smoky scent of ash and
burnt wood settles in my hair.
There is a small knot of people
clustered around Arthur's seat.
Elaine, Arthur's rich voice
startles me from
dark thoughts.
He approaches, his
eyes soft and tired.
Thank you for coming. I had
hoped you would help
Gwynivere, daughter of Lodengrance,
find her way here. I am afraid
the notion of living in a battle camp
is one wholly strange to her.
I look over at her, and she returns
my gaze with a cold stare,
her eyes following the creases of my
gown, lingering on the dirt
and grass stains at the hem.
I cannot help but think of a serpent

as I focus on her icy blue eyes.
They are hard, there is no warmth
or friendliness behind them.
I look back at Arthur.
I know you will be great friends,
he says, almost pleading.
Is it possible? Could this girl
be the female companion,
the friend
I have always wanted, dreamed of?
Her expression is aloof.
I do not feel very confident.
Of course, Arthur, I say to him.
I will do what you wish, my friend.
His eyes, so dark,
look moist, and something
swims behind them that
I have never seen there before.
　　　Hopelessness.
I wonder, is this how I look?
I thank you, Elaine, he whispers.

I wonder, could it be
that he does not wish to marry
Gwynivere? But she is so pretty?
Lancelot still stands beside Gwynivere.
And he still gazes
on her in the manner of a devoted
puppy dog doting on its master.
And she returns his look.
A stab of pain clutches me.
Gwynivere, please allow me to introduce
you to Elaine, daughter of Barnard of Ascolat,
and dear friend, Arthur begins.
She has lived among us for many years,
and perhaps can show you what she knows
of herbal medicines. For she is an
invaluable nurse and healer.
Gwynivere merely nods,
her long, golden tresses falling
smoothly down her shoulders.
Good, then. Arthur looks around
uneasily. *We shall leave you ladies*

alone.

Alone.

I can't think of anything

less good at this moment.

Arthur meets my eyes once more,

and then he touches Lancelot

on the shoulder. Lancelot

shakes his head, as though he shakes

himself awake from a dream, and the pair,

along with Lodengrance, my

father, and my brother turn

and leave, leave me alone

with Gwynivere.

What can I show you? I ask.

Surely Arthur spoke to you of the

Round Table, where you sit now.

     She sits, while I stand,

         waiting on her like a servant.

Gwynivere looks at me, then

down at her hands, which are

neatly folded in her lap.

Yes, he did, she replies stonily.
An awkward silence descends,
as I struggle to find a topic
for conversation.
Would you like to learn about the healing arts?
I stammer.
I have no interest in your plants.
The bitterness in her voice
takes me by surprise, more
than the harshness of her words.
Very well. I am unsure
of how to talk to her.
*Do you wish me to show
you the camp?*
Gwynivere looks bored,
and she looks down again
at the bottom of my dress,
her nose wrinkling in distaste.
*Nor have I any interest in tramping
through the mud and filth,
as you so clearly relish doing.*

I am not a beast, Elaine.
She pronounces my name
slowly, drawing it out,
each syllable dripping
with venom.
She thinks me a beast?
What have I done to her?
I am a stranger to her.
Do I look so rough,
so ugly and rough
that I seem so to her?
I can only gape at her, feeling
a red heat creep up my neck
and bloom across my cheeks.
She smirks at me,
a superior grin spreading
smugly over her lips.
You may show me my tent, she orders,
as though I were her servant.
How I long to leave her

there in the fire pit to find her own way,
but I know I cannot
disappoint Arthur.
Follow me, I sigh
and spin around and lead her
through the maze of tents,
to her own, which, as I peer
inside, I can see is littered
with rich, carmine rugs and
a sumptuous pallet stuffed with
fresh hay.
She brushes past me and slips
into her tent, letting the flaps fall
closed behind her, without a word
or a glance in my direction.
I let out a long breath and shake my head.
Was I mad to have wished for another
girl to keep me company all these years?
Morgan certainly does not behave
anything like Gwynivere.

My stomach twists and clenches again.
I wander through the tents,
as the weak sun, a dull
white spot in the sky,
begins to sink below the horizon.
The vision of Lancelot and Gwynivere's embrace
burns.
I cannot shake it away.
My birch trees tremble in the slight
breeze that slithers through the camp.
I slide between them, feeling the
bark, light and delicate,
on my fingers, the scent of dried
leaves soothing me.
The peace of this grove
feels almost magical,
as though some goddess of silver-barked
trees watches over me.
I lean against a slender trunk,
feeling the leaves playing in my hair,

and listen to the sound of my own breath.
For the first time since
the night my mother died,
I feel truly alone.

XXI

The men bustle around camp
like ants, checking to make
sure their weapons,
shields, provisions are
battle ready, journey ready.
They come by our tent,
sheepish looks on their faces,
bedraggled cloaks and tunics
in hand, holding them out like
offerings.
Elaine, do you think you might
have time to add a few stitches
before we are off?
Gawain, with Gaheris and Gareth in tow,
arrives at midday, a pile
of breeches and a hauberk
in hand.

Gawain bows his head slightly.
Elaine, I know all the boys must
be coming by with their rags,
but if you could find time to
help us with some mendin'
we would be mighty grateful.
Our breeches just need
a bit of stitchin' up, and my
hauberk here, well, a few
of the chain links have come
off. Do you think you could
patch them up?
Gawain looks like a small boy,
his eyes hopeful and bashful at once.
Well, I don't want some Saxon
poking holes in you, now, so I
will see what I can do about the
chain mail. I should be able to
sew them back on, I reassure him.
Leave it here. I will have it all
ready for you before you leave.

Really? Gawain's huge face lights up.
Thank you so much, Elaine,
we are forever in your debt.
Thank you, Elaine! Gaheris echoes.
Much indebted, Gareth calls over his shoulder.
And do not worry — I will report
back to you all that happens,
every blow of my sword,
every Saxon who begs for mercy.
I will bring back all of the news
to you.

He grins his oafish grin once
more, then the trio of brothers moves away.
It amazes me how alike they look,
how alike in nature they are.
As I look at the floor all around my
pallet, around the dining table
and benches, the mountains
of clothes awaiting mending
suddenly feel too overwhelming.
There is no possibility of my finishing

all of this before it is time to leave.
And how will I find the time to gather
all of the herbs I need?
I throw the armload of Gawain's and his
brothers' clothes on the floor in
a flare of temper.
It is so unfair that the task I hate
more than any other is the one my brothers
and friends have need of me for.
Why do you not ask the new girl?
Lavain's voice startles me from
my reverie.
What? I ask, surprised that
he has been in here with me all this
time and kept silent.
Ask Lodengrance's daughter to help you.
With the mending, he says.
I do not need her help, I reply,
my voice rising, despite my
efforts to keep calm.
What upsets you? Lavain

rises from his bed and comes to
stand before me.
All the work that weighs on you?
Or having someone to share it with?
Lavain, I know not what you speak of.
I will do the work, as I always have done,
I retort, feeling my face redden.
So it is sharing the work, then. He smirks.
I see no one here to share the
load with me, actually. My hands
begin to shake with anger. Why,
why do I let him irk me so?
As all of you would be running
about half naked with your guts
hanging out if I were not here
to fix the tears in your clothes
and in your flesh, I suggest you
keep quiet and leave me be.
Frustration is pulsing in my blood now.
I am going out to gather milfoil, I snap.
And I leave the piles of tunics

and breeches and cloaks and my brother,
who stares after me, mouth hanging
agape, and stamp outside.
My whole body trembles with rage.
What a dolt, I grunt, replaying the
exchange in my mind, as I stumble
away from the camp, find the
stepping-stones in the River Usk
and cross over to the moor
on the other side.
The wild grass grows long, and
small purple wildflowers dot the
landscape.
The world feels very large here.
Wide open.
Finally. Space to breathe.
I loosen my hair and let
it fall down my back. The wind
whips it around and it beats my
face. I grab a lock and wind
it around my fingers. The colors

of wheat and summer strawberries.
Nothing new or particularly interesting
there. It is not the color of flaxseeds
or faerie's gold. Not like hers.
Dull.
I fall to my knees, letting the
great sky press down on me.
I turn onto my back and stare up
at the heavens. There is not
a cloud to disturb the unending blue.
Blue.
Blue like water
and painted demons
and her eyes.
Blue like peaceful dreams
and freedom.
A pair of larks sweep into
view, black lines against the
sky. They swoop and play
and trill and fly away.
This is my home.

This dirt, this soil.
It is all I have and all I am.
No tent, no man,
no sewing needle to enclose
and imprison me.
Suddenly, the crunching of feet breaking
twigs and flower stalks.
I sit up quickly and spot a tall
figure some yards away.
He does not see me, no, he stands,
oblivious to the world.
It is Lancelot.
I crouch in the grass and watch him.
He stares out into the distance, unseeingly.
His profile perfect, his stance perfectly still.
I long to run to him, to throw my arms
around him,
even to tap his shoulder and prance away,
challenging him to a race
as I would have done
before,

before

she came.

I sit back and hug my knees.

Lancelot, I call out.

He turns quickly, his face

filled with joy and yearning,

then it falls, crumples as soon as

his eyes light on me.

No, I am not the one he hoped for.

Oh, hello, Elaine, he calls back,

his voice heavy and dull.

Come sit by me awhile, I ask,

my voice too cheery.

I know not what I am doing now.

He moves in my direction, as

though propelled by some outside

force.

What troubles you on this fine day,
Lancelot? The earth blesses us with all
her beauty today. Why do you not find
pleasure in her gifts?

His green eyes are dimmed,
and he keeps them on the horizon.
I have lost myself, he answers.
Lost yourself? But you are right here,
sitting beside me.
He does not respond, just stares.
She will marry him. Arthur, he says,
his voice filled with a bitter sorrow,
impenetrable and chilled. He continues,
Why does it have to be him? Of all men?
My best friend.
She should be mine.
But I will never have her.
Never. His voice breaks.
My little sparrow returns,
fluttering, frightened.
She beats as hard as my heart,
and I feel I might burst.
You could have me, I whisper.
The words just slip out.
I gasp and feel the blood drain

from my cheeks. I cannot believe
how I have spoken.
You? he asks, and his eyes are cold,
cruel. *You are naught but a child, Elaine.*
You would not understand.
My heart, what was left of it,
shatters. A thousand little pieces,
shattered and scattered over this
wild moor, seeded in the grasses.
I gasp, and turn away.
My body feels wooden and dead.
Lancelot does not turn to watch me.
He just stares out
into the distance.
Then I turn and run.

XXII

I run back to the river,
as if a wolf chases me for my life.
I imagine great, slavering fangs
nipping at my heels, and almost
wish it would devour me, but
I strip off my dress, loosening the
ties that bind it, and throw it to the ground,
and I dive into the river, letting the cold
water cover me. I push myself
down to the bottom, until I feel the slimy
rocks and silt dancing beneath my toes.
I puff out my cheeks and keep my breath
close, until I can hold it no more.
Then I glide upward to the surface and
take in a great mouthful of air.
As I turn to look around at the willow tree,
I notice a figure on the camp-side shore.

Gwynivere.
She is watching me closely, her
cornflower eyes
squinting against the sunlight.
What were you and Lancelot
talking about? she asks, her voice
filled with poison.
What do you care? I answer,
surprised by the loathing
in my own tone,
surely, it is none of your
concern.
You really are a beast,
Elaine, taking off your gown
and swimming like
some wild thing.
I flip onto my back and begin to
kick, propelling myself close
to where she stands and kicking
harder, splashing water
onto her feet.

Oh! You are horrid! she screams.

Yes, I reply, *I know. A wild beast.*

And I kick some more,

sending water droplets onto her dress.

Gwynivere moves backward a pace,

then sticks out her tongue at me

and runs back to camp.

Some lady you are! I call after her.

I swim to the opposite shore, and

shake the excess water from my arms

and legs. I pull on my dress,

which clings damply to my body,

then find my way back to the stepping-stones.

And I laugh to myself,

all the way to our tent,

until I remember that I did not bring

back any milfoil.

207

XXIII

The pile grows daily.
Every man in the camp
has brought me at least one piece
of clothing to mend.
I have no choice now,
but to ask for help.
To ask Gwynivere for help.
I try to string the right
words together, then
rehearse what I will say.
Gwynivere, I have too much
mending, and I fear —
No, I do not want to admit fear
to her.
I have much mending to do,
and need your help —
No, I do not want to admit to

needing her.

I approach her tent and

cough, hoping that will attract

her attention.

Who is there? Lance —

Her eyes, at first bright with

a smile, turn fiery.

Oh, it is you. What do you want?

Gwynivere, I do not know why

you hate me, but there is

too much mending to do for one person.

Will you help me?

She looks at me coolly, as if

weighing her options.

No, I do not think I will.

I care not for sewing, and find it

beneath me. Unless it is sewing a standard

for Arthur to bear into battle, do not

speak to me again of sewing.

She turns and lets the tent flap

fall closed in my face.

Fury heats my blood,
and I want to scream.
No one, not even Lavain,
has ever spoken to me the way she does.
No one.
Oh, how she fools all the men
with her pretty looks, her
fair skin and soft hands and
luminous eyes.
A gown woven by faeries
could not disguise her cruel nature.
But I do not know how to respond,
and as these thoughts,
and —
and my jealousy
     yes, jealousy
wheel through
my mind, my tongue sticks
in my mouth, as though a little
jaybird has flow in and caught
it like a worm.

I hate her. My tongue is unloosed suddenly.
I am shocked by this evil, black
feeling that fills my gut.
I have never felt such,
such hate before.
Whom do you hate? Tristan is beside me.
*Tristan, you are like a ghost! I hate how
you sneak up on me,* I snap.
Instantly his friendly expression
droops.
I am sorry, I sigh. *I just —*
Whom do you hate? he asks again,
the smile returning to his eyes.
No one, I grumble.
*No one with long yellow hair and
gowns far too fancy
for an army encampment?*
he teases.
I can only stare at him agog.
How did you know? I breathe.
Well, I have never seen such an

expression on your face, in all the years
that I have known you.
I see where you stand,
and so, I figured, it must be
the newest addition to our happy camp.
I sigh. *Yes, well,*
you guessed correctly. I
do not understand it, Tristan. She is
so remarkably cruel to me.
I am seething again.
Yes? Well, then I hate her too, Tristan says.
What do I do? I cannot be her friend;
she has no interest in friends, I shout.
Unless that friend is Lancelot.
Or Arthur, I suppose. I cannot
catch my breath. *But this I also*
do not understand: She flirts openly with
Lancelot, yet everyone knows she is betrothed
to Arthur. How can she behave so brazenly?
My face is red, I can feel it.
Tristan is suddenly serious again.

I cannot tell how things will end, but
this friendship — *Gwynivere and Lancelot's* —
it does not bode well. I like it not, he says.
Though Arthur seems not to notice . . .
or not to care, I add.
Yes, I have noticed his not noticing, as well,
Tristan says, thoughtfully. *I cannot imagine*
how he could possibly be blind to it. Perhaps —
perhaps there is another reason. Perhaps
he does not care whether
Lancelot and Gwynivere flirt under
his own nose. Tristan strokes his chin.
Well, anyway, what do we do about this
would-be princess? Tristan asks, grinning wolfishly.
What do we do? I ask, confused. *What can we do?*
Oh, there are lots of things, he answers
mischievously. *Do we know what she*
is afraid of? We can give Lady Gwynivere
a gift, a small token of our
appreciation, if you will.
Perhaps she likes frogs, or worms,

or mice, or ——

Tristan looks around at the
ground happily, as though searching
for some creepy-crawly inspiration.
How about a small, brown toad? I interrupt,
thinking of how I felt the day I met her.
In her bed? Tristan finishes.
We look at each other, then turn around
and head back to the river.
When we have a small toad in our possession,
trembling in Tristan's closed fist,
we sneak back to camp, ready to keep
our prisoner in an improvised jail cell
of sticks and leaves.
But as we pass the Round Table, we
come upon Arthur, Lodengrance, and
Gwynivere in conference.
Her tent is empty, Tristan whispers.
Now is our moment. Come!
We tiptoe over to her tent, and as
Tristan holds back the flap, I

enter, looking for a place to
deposit the toad.

How about on her pillow? Tristan asks.

*No! It will escape. We need a better
place,* I hiss, shaking my head.

Ah, here! I find her small
embroidery bag. *This is perfect.*

Will she look in it tonight? he asks.

I am sure of it, I answer.

We slide our small, slimy soldier
into the silken purse and draw the
strings tight.

Now he cannot hop away, Tristan
murmurs, then he grabs my hand,
and we race out of the tent into the
evening air.

We are laughing so hard now, that tears
are streaming down my cheeks, and my side
aches with cramps.

I have not felt so light and
carefree in days.

215

Then a piercing scream shatters the
gathering dusk.
And Tristan and I begin to laugh again,
harder, even, than before.
Shhh, he gasps, taking my hand
once more and pulling me toward
the shiver of birches.
We collapse to the ground together,
still chuckling.
Tristan's eyes are closed and
he still clutches my hand in his own.
Tristan, I whisper, easing my hand from his grasp.
Elaine? He opens his eyes slowly,
and they are startlingly light, almost yellow.
Did you know your eyes change colors?
I ask him, bringing my hand to his temple,
then staying myself.

                              What am I doing?

Did you know yours do too?
They change from grey to green to brown,
the colors of the forest,

the colors of the sky,

Tristan replies softly.

I have never seen a green sky, I giggle.

No? he asks, suddenly serious.

Before a summer storm,

the sky turns green, green like your eyes.

He reaches a hand into his pocket. *Elaine,*

he whispers, *I — I wanted to give you something,*

before we left. I was not sure —

Tristan's voice grows rough.

Here, these are for you.

He grabs my hand again and turns

it so my palm faces up.

Then he lays something slick and heavy

on it.

I look down and gasp.

Tristan, it is beautiful.

A necklace, two strands

of delicately carved wooden

beads, gleams like ivory in the moonlight.

It is perfect, I tell him. *Thank you.*

You are welcome, Tristan mumbles quietly.

He holds my gaze, then turns away abruptly.

It grows late. Your father will wonder

where you are. Come, I shall escort you

to your tent.

He pulls me to my feet, and we walk

in silence as the night folds

into a deep shade of violet around us.

Good night, he whispers at the mouth

of my tent.

Tristan — ? I begin, but

he is gone.

XXIV

I lay down to
sleep, the beads resting
beside me on my pillow,
I stroke them. They are smooth
and cool.
I call up the sound
of Gwynivere's scream;
it reverberates in my head.
I behaved like a child.
Worse, a cruel child.
My mother would be so
ashamed; I am so ashamed.
I feel my face
burning
in the dark.
I want to scream.
I want to scream, because

it is not me.

This is not Elaine of Ascolat.

She does not play mean, childish
pranks.

I reach for my shawl, my fingers
shaking.

I will walk in the night.

Stars fill the black, black sky,
dusty and brilliant.

The air is cool and soft,
like a mother's hands,
soothing.

When I look up at the heavens,
it is hard to believe that everything
down here on this earth is changing,
so fast, so terribly.

Everyone I know and love is about to
march into war, about to start a war.

Finish it.

How can they just turn their backs
on me and march away,

not knowing if they will ever
come back
to me?
I plan to follow, yes
but they do not know it.
How can they do it?
How can my brothers and my father
leave me all alone?
My vision is blurred as
tears fill my eyes,
and I clutch Tristan's necklace
in my hands, rubbing the
beads between my fingers.
Of course, they are men,
and they do what is practical,
without a thought for what
or whom they leave behind.
The birch trees loom ahead
like a brotherhood
of silver silent ghosts.
Last year's leaves smell fresh

and I drift among the trees,
myself a silver silent ghost in
the moonlight.
Everything in this world changes
given the passage of enough time.
And what will be if Arthur succeeds?
I dare not even think on it.
The peace that we all hope for,
that they fight for,
gathers on the horizon
like a brewing storm.
This peace would leave us
scattered and apart.
Will we Ascolats return to our
island? We have no home
left on Shalott.
I do not even know where Lancelot
comes from.
Where will he go?
And Arthur and Gwynivere?

Still, the peace that we all pray for,
it is our only hope.

I scan the moon
for a glimpse of the goddess face,
for a sign of what is to come,
but all I can see is
Lancelot's face, Arthur's face,
Tirry's and Lavain's and my father's,
Tristan's face.
And they look frightened.
When everything changes,
what will be at the end of everything?
O Lord.
O Mistress of the Moon.
I know not whom to ask
for guidance.
At the end of all of this,
  will I find myself alone?

XXV

Sunlight filters through the
hide of the tent, wresting me from
a dreamless slumber.
Once again I am alone, and
once my chores are finished,
I carry an armload of clothes
outside, down to the river,
where I find a seat on a bed
of clover, below the great
elm tree.
There, I take up my mending.
It is better to do by the light
of the sun than squinting in the
gloomy shade of the tent.
As I stitch a gaping hole in
Gawain's breeches, the river
babbles and burbles past.

All is quiet and still. There is
no wind to move the tree's branches,
nor to rustle the grasses and reeds
that line the river's banks.
Then a twig snaps, and I
look up from my task to see
Arthur striding toward me.
His features are haggard,
lines I never noticed before,
standing out around his eyes.
Hello, I call to him, letting
the needle and pants fall into my lap.
I thought I might find you here.
You seem to favor the company of
trees to men, these days. Arthur
runs a quick hand through his curly
brown locks, and looks at me,
his eyes squinting,
as though he gauges
my mood.
Trees are solid, dependable;

they can be trusted, I reply.
Unlike men, Arthur finishes, sitting
beside me.
Most men, I add.
I do not know, Elaine.
Even those of us with the best
of intentions can be unreliable,
weak. His eyes grow dark.
Arthur, I say gently, *let us not*
talk of such things. The sun
shines and the sparrow sings.
Uncertain days lie ahead,
but for now, let us enjoy what
is certain and wonderful.
And he is silent,
staring out over the river,
lost in his own thoughts.
There is no time for regrets
or sorrow, I tell him,
in these days of war.

Yes, you are right, I suppose,
he agrees,
but I cannot help but wonder
if —
if all my arranging
and concocting and
planning is leading me,
us —
all of us —
astray.
The very existence of Britain,
all of Britain rests on this
scheme, and who am I to
presume that I can —
that I can lead?
So many lives,
so very many lives
are in my hands.
What if the Merlin's prophecy
is false?

I cannot help but be fearful.
Arthur's confession startles
my own worries from my head.
Oh, Arthur, you must not
doubt yourself. You are meant to
lead us, to fight for Britain and to
take her back from the invaders
who would enslave us.
You must never question that.
All you believe in is right and pure.
The men follow you because they know
in their hearts this is true,
I tell him, *and you must believe it too.*
What would I do without your good counsel,
Elaine? He looks at me then
looks down at the ground.
A-hem!
We both look up as a cough
startles us both from our thoughts.
Gwynivere approaches, a cold sneer
curling her lips.

Hello, Gwynivere. Arthur rises,
and gives a short bow of his head.
Good day, sir, she addresses him,
ignoring me. *My father bade me*
to aid in gathering herbs and plants.
She looks at him demurely. *Of course,*
I told him, I do all that I can to aid
in the cause. In your cause.
Arthur glances down at me,
an uneasy blush spreading over his
cheeks. *Yes, well, Elaine, I am sure,*
will show you which plants
bear the necessary fruits, so to speak.
You will guide Gwynivere, will you not, Elaine?
But of course, Arthur, I respond,
my head buzzing with rage. The gall,
the staggering, dishonest gall!
Arthur is still looking at me,
probably wondering why my face
has twisted itself into a grimace of
fury.

Come, Gwynivere. Let us hunt for
red clover. It is good for poultices
to stop inflammation.
Thank you, Elaine. Arthur looks
relieved and abashed at once.
Good! I think.
But it is not his fault, I remind
myself. He is as much a victim
of circumstances as I am.
More so, perhaps, as he does
his duty and is paid in this way
for it.
Good day, ladies, he says, then
swiftly lopes away.
What does this wretched weed look like?
Gwynivere's tone is icy.
The flower varies from violet to crimson,
and the leaves are ragged and hairy.
They grow this tall, I explain,
motioning to the middle of my calf.

Follow me, I sigh, leaving my mending,
and leading her down
to the river, where, gingerly, I step
across the slippery stones that
lead to the other shore.
They grow here, on the moor.
But she is not listening to me,
her forehead creased with
consternation. Gwynivere lifts her
skirts and balances shakily
on the rocks.
If you walk quickly, you will stand
a better chance of not falling in, I warn.
Hmph, she grunts. *We cannot*
all be wild things like you.
Remembering the brown toad
I slipped in her embroidery bag,
I remind myself I have treated her
badly enough, in spite of her cruel words.
Still, I cannot help but grit my teeth.

I am stalking through the meadow grasses,
trying to calm my nerves, tearing
the clover from the ground when I see it.
I glance back to make sure Gwynivere
has not drowned, and I see her standing
on the near bank, stiff as a stone statue.
The grass does not bite! I call, and I hold
up a stem of clover, waving the
plum-colored blossom in the air.
And this is what you are to pick.
Try not to bring me any ragwort.
We move without speaking, though once
in a while, I hear her stumble and yelp,
or mutter in frustration.
Her heavy pink gown,
with all its layers,
must be sweltering
in the springtime sunshine.
I begin to pity her; clearly she has never
spent time wandering in the fields.
You must be warm, I call to her. *You may*

take off your gown. I promise I will not
look. I can feel a satisfied smirk
playing on my lips.
She only harrumphs in response.
But I spot her watching me with envy
in her eyes, as I remove my dress,
and lay it flat over a rock, so that I may
wander about in just my shift,
lighter and much cooler.
Really, it is quite comfortable, Gwynivere!
I tease.
Fine! she screams, startling a flock of
meadowlarks. She attacks the laces of
her dress viciously, and jerks the gown
over her head, only to get stuck
and flail about, trapped inside the
multitude of folds and bunches of material.
She stumbles around in a short circle,
and I giggle, then run toward her, ready to help.
Gwynivere, I say, putting out a hand to stop her.
Gwynivere — but she continues to twist and

wrench from my grasp.

Gwynivere! Stop! Let me help you.

I can tell she is reluctant to let me
aid her, but she halts and I grab
two handfuls of the abundant fabric
and pull the gown over her
head.

Gwynivere seizes the gown from
my hands, snapping it back,
as though I were trying to steal it from her.

I look at her, waiting for thanks, but
none comes.

She spins on her heel and bends to the ground,
snatching a knot of grass and a single
clover head.

Very well, I say, and turn away,
returning to my own gathering.

Now, however, the silence between
us feels less charged, somehow. Easier.

Perhaps I have found a chink
in her armor?

I am through here, she shouts at me.
This is a servant's work. You may finish it.
And she throws her gown over her
arm and storms away, back to the river.
How wrong I was, I murmur, reeling
a bit, though I am unsure why.
Why do I still feel surprised by
her intolerable rudeness? I wonder.
At least I will not be lingering
here for much longer, I whisper to the meadow.
Soon enough, I will bid you a silent farewell too.
And I don my dress and follow Gwynivere
back across the river,
back to the camp.

XXVI

As I near our tent,
the sounds of clanging swords
and grunting men find my ears.
The soldiers are still at work,
which gives me time to begin
packing away all that I will need
for my journey.
The other night,
I overheard Tirry and my father
discussing the march in hushed tones.
It is to last five days and five nights,
stretching over rough country,
forest, hills, and swamp.
We will move to the east, across a mighty river,
and then to the south, until we reach
the fort of Cerdic Strong-in-the-Arm,

that beastly Saxon who leads the invaders,
Tirry described.

I bring my mother's chest and take from
it the silvered glass.
My eyes, as murky and muddy as ever,
look older to me, somehow.
I cannot say what it is that has changed,
exactly, but these eyes I do not
recognize.
Again I ask myself,
Am I beautiful?
Do I look like a woman now?
Lancelot's words echo in my head,

> *You? You are naught but a child, Elaine.*
> *You would not understand.*

I shudder at the memory
of his sneering disdain.
Naught.

                    I must be ugly.

I tuck the glass back
into the chest, beneath the
linens and pretty
white things.
Then I pull out the leaves and flowers
and seeds I secreted away earlier,
the bits of cheese and dried fruit,
nuts and crusts of bread,
and I spread everything from my cache
onto the table.
There is not much.
Not nearly enough.
Not for five days and five nights,
and certainly not for more than that.
I will have to do better.
And how will I carry all of it?
As I finger the ruffled sheets
and napkins, an idea takes shape.
I lift one soft, white linen sheet
from the chest,
shaking it open.

Yes, that will do.
I recover my needle from a man's
stained and ratty tunic, and a
length of woolen thread, and begin to sew
the edges of the sheet together,
closing it up like a sack.
Carefully I wrap the plants
in leather pouches.
I have already prepared
poultices and tinctures for the
men to carry with them,
but I will feel more
confident knowing that
I bear more medicines
that I can prepare myself
when I am with them.
From the pantry, I collect some smoked meat,
more cheese, and a loaf
of bread. A flagon of cider.
This will have to do.
I tuck all of the provisions

into the sack and cover it all with
my cloak.
A shiver runs through me.
As I plan to march
toward battle and the unknown,
just as the men do, I wonder,
do I seek glory too?
It will be an adventure, and I have always
wanted, dreamed of having an adventure.
Again, a shiver,
 one of delight,

  excitement,
travels up my spine.
As I tuck the cotton sack back
into the trunk, I see a dark
shape moving against the flap of the tent.
Did I really see it?
Was someone spying on me?
Did somebody see me?
I duck my head outside, but no one is there.
I must have imagined it.

Still, the sense that someone was lurking,
watching, gnaws at me.
No, I must have imagined it.
I survey the room to be sure I
do not leave behind any evidence of my designs,
then lay myself to sleep.

XXVII

The men make ready to set out at dawn,
when the glow of the newborn sun
is sickly and pale.
My father kneels by the edge of my pallet;
his lips, warm and rough, gently
touch my forehead.
Daughter, he whispers.
I sit up quickly, startled.
I slept without hearing his
and my brothers' movements.
Surprised that I could sleep
knowing that I would be on my way,

                                  alone

too.
Father, I reply. *It is time?*
Yes, I am afraid so, dearest one.
My heart begins to beat fast,

too fast.

I cannot believe that all of these days

of planning have left me,

on the day itself, so unprepared.

And frightened.

Do not be afraid, my love, he says.

The fear must be seared across my face.

We will return to you soon.

My father's callused fingers

tickle my cheek,

and I throw my arms around his neck.

Father, I —

I break down into sobs,

I do not want you to go.

I do not want any of you to go.

This is madness . . . my voice breaks,

and I cannot speak anymore.

Shh, Elaine, hush, and do not cry.

We will be back before the next moon.

It is not so much time.

And Tirry and Lavain will take care of me,

you will see, no harm will find us.

His voice is softer than I remember

ever hearing it before.

I cry silently into the crook of his neck,

memorizing his smoky scent.

He reaches behind him and

unlocks my hands, laying them down

at my sides.

It is time, he echoes.

Say good-bye to your brothers,

and wish them well. For we are off.

I rise and embrace Tirry, who stands

two paces behind our father,

his face set in grim lines.

His blue eyes bore deep into mine,

and he grasps me by my shoulders,

holding me away from him.

All will be well, he intones.

I promise. Think on us with love

and good wishes. We shall see

each other soon. I feel it.

I nod and fight to hold back
fresh tears that threaten to
pour from my eyes. I feel
I could flood our little tent if
I allow myself to continue weeping.
Tirry, I whisper, thinking of the blood on
his cloak, *please be careful.*
We embrace once more, and then he
and my father leave the tent, and Lavain
and I are left alone. He
stands resolutely next to the
opening, his eyes
trained on the dirt floor.
Lavain. I hate
how my voice trembles
when I speak his name.
Lavain, I repeat. *Brother —*
I hate how I do not know what
to say to him.
He looks up at me, his eyes
steely and unreadable.

Please, I continue, *be watchful.*
And be — be well.
Lavain nods and takes a step
toward me. *Sister,* he says,
his voice a low growl, *we will*
return to you. And he is gone.
There is no touch, no pat of reassurance.
No gesture, no word of love
or affection, yet, somehow,
I know he meant as much.
I run outside the tent and my three
men turn back to me and raise
their hands in silent farewell,
as I feel the sky, in its leaden greyness,
fall down upon me.
I sink to my knees,
crying and praying.
Please, O Lord, please, Goddess of the Moon,
keep them safe, I beg.
I wait until they vanish into the pearly mist
that seems a cousin to the dawn.

Then I run back into the tent and
pull my white linen sack from
my mother's chest,
my sparrow flapping her wings, as what
I am about to do
sinks in.
I replace the linens,
carefully folding them.
The danger of what I am
about to attempt seizes me,
and I wonder, will I ever see
this chest again?
I reach down to the bottom of the
coffer and pull out a small lace
cloth — my mother's handkerchief.
I stuff that into the sack too,
and again, as I reach into the box
to straighten the materials that are
left, my fingers brush something hard and
cold. Tristan's necklace.
I withdraw the strands of beads that

I had stored in the trunk for safekeeping,
and fasten them around my neck.
His strange but lovely gift feels
like an amulet for protection.
That is all. I close the chest
and walk out of the tent,
looking back just once.
Will I come back?
Will I survive?
I know not. Nor do I know
of another choice.
And so I begin walking,
following the track of
foot- and hoofprints, following
the distant sound of horses
whinnying and feet and hooves
pounding the earth.

XXVIII

The sun is high overhead,
and I am walking north and east.
I am still following the tracks in the mud,
praying that I do not lose them.
The leaves of so many trees
make lacy patterns against the slate-colored
sky, and I worry that it will soon rain.
I have no shelter, no skins with which
to cover myself. I did not plan as well
as I thought.
Birds call to one another
in the morning sky, and I sing
to myself to keep
my thoughts from wandering to Lancelot.
It is useless.
The last words we exchanged on the moor,
his icy glare.

You? he sneered.

How small and ugly I feel
at just the memory of it,
the way his lips curled,
and his voice rose and trembled.
Then I remember his promise
of pearls and that sweet night
by the fire, that night that
was filled with so much
promise.

As my thoughts drift from one
place to the next, the sun, too,
drifts from one point to the next.
I am starting to feel tired, and
I must keep my mind focused
on moving my feet forward and forward,
watching the trail, keeping the mountains
ever behind me and to the south.

At times I get the oddest sensation
that someone is following me,
watching me from the line of trees

to the west.

Nay, it cannot be.

The sickly sun now hides

behind grey wisps of clouds,

and sweat begins to bead

above my upper lip, along my brow.

My boots are sturdy but I can

feel a blister forming on the big toe

of my right foot, and the sack

grows heavier and heavier.

I am lonely. Lonely and an

emptiness gnaws at me.

There are no more birdcalls; I can hear

nothing but the wind in the grasses

and in the trees. And the faint sound of my feet

tamping down the earth,

a mockery of the heavy, pounding marching

of the men.

Thunder rumbles in the distance

like an angry beast preparing to charge.

Drops of rain, fat and juicy,

fall from the sky,
splashing over my nose
and eyelashes.
The rain comes slowly at first,
but soon it is pouring from the sky.
I must stop.
A small stand of oak trees lies
some paces away, and I run for the
cover of their great branches.
As I huddle beneath one of the oaks,
the thick smell of wet leaves
and earth reminds me of my
mother's tower room, so far away now,
on the isle of Shalott.
A wound in one of the tree trunks
exposes golden white flesh that
reminds me of that oaken loom,
gleaming in sunlight and crowned by shadows.
That loom bore the scars of time and love
and use, my mother's wisdom,
her gentleness and care.

Thunder and lightning crash
above my head, and for an instant I wonder
if the tree that shelters me will be
brought down by the raging forces
of the storm.
The sky is nearly black, but an eerie
glow signals that night has not yet fallen.
With each blast of thunder, my heart thuds
a little faster. With each bolt of lightning
forking across the sky, I curse my
decision to make this journey on my own.
No one will even know if I die here.
I am so alone.
I have always been alone.
      No,
that is not true.
The faces of Lancelot, Lavain,
Tirry, Father, Arthur, Tristan, and Morgan —
those who have been with me — float
inside my eyelids.
They have been with me, since —

since she died.

The rain is letting up now,

and the sky turns a greenish grey.

My clothes, my hair, my sack, everything

is soaked. Everything feels

so much heavier than it did before the storm.

My breath catches, as I look all around

for the trail.

I cannot find it.

I turn this way and that,

panic filling my limbs,

making them tight and shaky.

Has the rain washed away the path?

No, it is there.

I simply did not walk far enough.

The mud is churned up and slippery;

giant puddles filled with brown water make

for treacherous stepping.

Birds call to each other:

Come, find your supper and come to bed.

I march and march, the trees and

grass and sky all green and grey.
And the green grows
greyer as dusk approaches.
An owl shrieks and the whisper of
wings overhead sends my heart racing.
As darkness closes in, the loneliness
feels like it might overwhelm me.
The sky is black now, and the spray of stars
can barely be seen through the thick clouds.
I want my father, the warmth of his embrace,
the pressure of his hand on my arm.
Even Lavain's teasing would be
welcome now — anything to stave
off the loneliness.
I can feel the trail, where the earth has been
torn apart and battered by so many feet
before mine. But fear is crawling up my throat;
I may choke.
The silhouette of a hulking tree trunk looms
up ahead, on the side of the path.
I shall sleep beneath its sheltering branches

tonight.
I spread my cloak over the wet ground,
squirming and wishing for my
dry bed.
I do not want to build a fire
and attract the attention of Arthur
and his men,
or anybody else for that matter,
though I likely could not find
a scrap of dry kindling, anyway.
The night is so dark.
I can hardly see my hand before my face,
and I feel eyes on me,
nevertheless.
Evil eyes,
hungry eyes.
I do not know how I will ever
find sleep.
Twigs snap, leaves rustle,
and stirrings come from

the tall grasses. I do not want
to meet what is out there.
I wish it were not a new moon,
but there is no relief from the
darkness.

XXIX

Morning fades
into afternoon
into dusk.
The sun rises
and sets, then a sliver
of a crescent moon
takes her place in the sky.
And I just walk and walk,
following a path left by those
who walked this land before me.
The late spring grass is green as a
frog's back, and trees line up
like an army of old friends,
urging me on.
Now I have taken to greeting the larks
and jays as they hunt for worms,
wishing the elm and linden trees well

as they wave to me in the breeze.
They and the tiny brown field mice who
sometimes dart across my path
are my only company.
Still the sense that someone
watches me stays with me.
Of course my mind wanders
often.
It wanders back to Lancelot,
and I remember how his green
eyes bored into mine the day
we met by the river.
How much hope I had that day,
how my heart lifted, took wing
when he told me

    I was beautiful.
Then I remember how quick he was
to trample it, to crush it
that day in the meadow.
Will my heart ever stop aching
at the memories of how

much I loved him,

how coldly he looked on me,

how scornful his voice,

his words were?

Words

words.

One word.

Gwynivere.

Why has she

come and ruined

everything?

Morgan's voice fills my head,

One never knows what

fate holds in store.

Up ahead a river, a river

separating the west country from

the swampy summer lands, a river

thick as a sea monster's tail.

And I must cross it.

No horse to carry me over,

no one to catch me
if I should drown.
I take off my dress and shoes
and stuff them into
my linen pack, then I raise
the sack over my head
and begin to wade into
the water. The current
is fast and the stones
beneath my feet are slippery.
With my arms above my head,
my balance is shaky, and
my ankles wobble as I make my
way toward the center of the river.
The murky green water
reaches my knees,
my hips, my chest, and then —
my feet slide, my toes scrambling
to catch hold of a rock, any perch,
but the water is rushing, rushing
past me, over me, begging to sweep me

away, down its merciless path.
Begging and pulling and
squeezing and sweeping, and
that icy cold, merciless water
catches me up in its current.
I cannot swim free. The water is savage,
white with foam as it tumbles
over rocks, tossing me, as though
I were no more than
a leaf, against a great, grey stone
that rises out of the water like a jagged tooth.
My arm is crushed between my
body and the rock; it burns
with pain. Tears spring to my eyes,
and water fills my throat.
Choking, blinded, I struggle to catch
hold of the stone, something.
My fingers are warm and sticky,
and I put them to my lips,
the iron taste of blood lingering
on my tongue.

I try to catch my breath,
but the water is relentless,
I do not know how much longer
I can hold on.
I look around.
If I could just get downriver
without being mashed against
the rocks, there is a point,
a lone point, where the land
juts out, and the river narrows,
and I would be able to cross
to the eastern shore.
But there is just one chance,
to swerve to the east,
toward the tooth of land.
If I miss it, surely, I will
be swept away
or crushed to death.
Slowly, reluctantly, I let go of
the grey rock I cling to,
allowing the furious current

to take hold of me once more.
I can barely keep my head up;
the sack has long since fallen below the
surface.
The current buoys me up and
spins me around lazily, like a polliwog.
But, surely enough, as I work my
way downstream, scraping against
rocks and fallen tree branches,
I am able to steer myself
to the far bank.
Gasping and spitting, I finally
feel my feet brush the bottom
of the river floor.
The satchel clutched to my chest,
I fight to wade out of the river
that nearly snatched away my life.

XXX

Four more days of
walking, alone in my head,
with memories of Lancelot and
Lavain and Tristan and Tirry
tumbling together like grains
of sand in the sea. I am nearing
the place, the place where a great
battle will be fought. I can feel it.
I can hear it. The drums of war
begin to throb, faintly,
so faintly. But with each step,
each silent footfall, the drums
grow louder, beats of a stick
on skin, and my heartbeat pulses
a frightened echo. For they are
Saxon drums.

XXXI

As I have drifted south,
I no longer know how far I am
from the mountain called Badon,
nor how many days of marching lay
ahead of me.
The loneliness sits heavily on my chest.
I think about how I nearly died doing what
men helping men, with a hand,
a strong shoulder, an outstretched arm
could have accomplished with ease.
But as evening draws near, I
can see smoke. Have I already caught
up with Arthur's army? Perhaps,
losing my way in the river
was fortunate after all?
I know not, but I stay quiet
and do not build my own fire.

I find shelter on a mossy bed beneath
an ash tree. Humming a tune
I have heard hummed a hundred
times in the camp, the melody Tristan
last played on his harp at the
Round Table, I feel home again,
closer to those I love and those
who love me.
And the wicked eyes of nighttime
do not frighten me as much.
The moon is clear and almost a quarter full,
and she is like an old friend.
My mother used to pray to God,
but Morgan told me there is a Goddess,
and the moon is her bauble. I know not
what to believe — what I believe —
but the moon is kind and a
kindred spirit.
The rustlings and the chirruping
of small, nighttime creatures
build to a crescendo until I fall asleep.

XXXII

Just one day more, and by
the rise of the moon, I think I should
arrive at Arthur's camp.
The drums are louder now,
pounding and pulsing fearsomely.
An angry beast has awoken,
of that there can be no doubt.
The Saxons have come in too
far, too near the heart of this land.
But I know our army will drive them out,
back to the eastern seas.
Still, those drums make my blood
freeze, and even my lips
feel cold with fear.
A chill creeps up and
down my spine; I could
swear there were eyes on me.

I wonder if there is some
terrible beast lurking in the
forest. Wolves have been
known to haunt this country.
But I cannot shake the sense that
something tracks me, following me
with its eyes, just some steps away.
Lurking and readying to pounce.
There is a rustle in the trees.

My blood is not all that is frozen.
My feet will not carry me a step farther,
and though I am begging them to move,

                             please,

please just another step,
please just lift and run,
please don't —
ah —
a hand on my shoulder,
not a paw or teeth or claws.
A hand.

It spins me and I nearly fall down,
as I meet the hard blue eyes
of a man I have never seen before.
His strange dress, furs, and skins
hanging from a belt about his waist,
long yellow hair hanging in
filthy ropes about his face —
a Saxon.
He throws his ugly head
back and lets out a grunting
call, *Wif!*
Two more men step out
of the trees like ghosts.
How long have they been tracking me?
Have I led them to Arthur?
The first man with the yellow hair
and mean eyes grabs my neck,
with his free hand, pulling my head back
a long knife flashing in his
hand.
A burning pain slides down my arm.

He has cut my arm,
and warm blood trickles down my
hand, falling in droplets onto the ground.
I can feel my throat closing again,
dread rising, panic, my heart
beating faster than the cursed drums.
The men are talking to one
another, their tones guttural and harsh.
Their eyes glitter like snakes',
oily and cruel.
I cannot breathe,
I do not think I can —

                                    stand.

My knees tremble and
I am sinking.
The Saxon grabs my hair,
I scream
like an animal.
Caught like an animal.
A deer
        to be slaughtered.

Blood pouring down my arm.
I will be lucky if that is
all they do to me.
My mind is running
too fast
too fast.
The Saxon drags me
by my hair,
and a keening moan
drags from my lips.
There is more rustling
and a scream.
Suddenly something flies from the trees,
in a rage,
like a wildcat,
fists flying,
scratching the Saxon who
holds me.
A clump of red hair
falls to the ground,
a red stain like blood

on the grey dust.
A puddle of blood,
no, my hair,
it is my hair.
And my blood.
Ropes of yellow hair fly and
whip my face, and I am lying
on the ground,
beside my pool of blood.
No, that is my hair.
I blink and see a familiar
figure above me.

Gwynivere?
Does she — does she
truly stand before me?
Is she real?
Gwynivere? I breathe.
She spins around and stares
at me.
She should not have turned,
for the three Saxons pounce on her.

Now they are the lions.

How did she get here?

Get up, she hisses while
struggling to break free of the
grasp of three dirty lion men,
who will certainly kill us both.

I am Arthur's wife! Gwynivere screams,
spitting in the face of the
yellow-haired Saxon.

One of the men grabs her
hand, and there is a gold
ring on her fourth finger.

Where did it come from?

What is happening?

She is his sister! Gwynivere
shrieks, her voice scratchy
and torn. *He will kill you all
if you hurt us.*

I try to raise myself,
but my eyes fall on my hair,
and I vomit.

Yellow bile
red hair
yellow hair
red blood.
I begin to wretch,
and I am crying too.
Get up, Elaine! she screams.
Gwyn — Gwynivere?
I cannot speak but to
whisper her name.
Elaine, stand up! she snaps.
And I stand.
My knees still shake,
but I am up on two legs,
and the world is spinning like mad.
Suddenly all is still, and I
am moving fast,
faster than a wildcat,
and I leap at dirty Yellow Hair,
my fingers claws,
tearing at his beard

and ropy locks,

an animal scream curls from my throat,

and I am breathing and snorting,

and blood is rushing through my head,

down my arm.

I see a river of red run down

the side of his face,

a river of blood,

red like my hair on the muddy ground.

He yelps and clutches his cheek.

I am kicking and

screaming and scratching,

and Gwynivere

is attacking the others,

and we are a tangle of yellow

and red and scratches and

arms and fingernails.

The knife clatters to the ground.

One of the men grabs me,

forces my arms to my sides.

I am breathing and writhing.

A beast caught in a snare.
Another has taken hold of Gwynivere,
her arms pinned to her sides also.
The men bark at each other
in their ugly language that sounds
like coughs and choking,
ugly words issuing
from spit-flecked lips,
yellow teeth flashing dangerously.
I am shaking with hate and
fury, and they begin to walk,
Yellow Hair pushing me ahead
of him, the others following,
with Gwynivere in the middle.
We march silently, though I can
hear Gwynivere breathing heavily.
Is she crying?
My tears have stopped, perhaps
I have cried my eyes dry.
The scenery passes too quickly,
all mottled

green and grey; a cloud seems
to have settled over my sight.
A sorry collection of flaccid,
ash-colored tents lies ahead,
and beyond them,
a steep hill. This must be the hill
called Badon.
I twist my head back to look at
Gwynivere. Her head hangs low,
her flaxen hair covering her face.
Is she hurt?
We approach the tents, and
more filthy men clad in
leather jerkins, with limp,
dirty skins and furs swinging
from their waists, appear.
Our captors grunt to them,
the others grunt back,
staring at Gwynivere and me
in a way that makes my skin
creep and shudder.

I know what Saxons do to women.
What will happen to us?
One man steps forward to
greet our party. He and Yellow Hair
speak, and I do not understand
a word they utter.
Then, the man from the tents bends
down to look in my eyes.
Sister of Arthur, we will hold you
prisoner, and we will keep you
until this battle is won.
Then, Arthur will pay for you.
No harm will come to you.
For now . . .
He grins a terrible grin,
yellow-and-black teeth
gleaming dully, and he turns
swiftly, and our captors push us
after him.
We stop in front of one of
the tents, the stink of dead animal

filling my nostrils,
filling my mouth with sour bile.
I retch and vomit again.
A sharp shove from behind,
and Yellow Hair screams angrily,
my vomit has fallen on his boots,
and I am tumbling into the tent.
Gwynivere stumbles in after me,
and Yellow Hair snarls at the man
who was holding her, and he follows us
into the tent, grabbing my wrist and
Gwynivere's, and dragging us to the center
pole. He forces us to the floor,
twisting my hand painfully. I try not
to make a sound, but a pitiful yelp
escapes, and he grabs my other wrist,
dropping Gwynivere's, and binds my hands
to the support pole.
My injured arm is throbbing, and my wrist
burns. Gwynivere is thrown down opposite
me, and her hands are also tied to the pole.

We are left to face each other, mute
with horror and fear.
The Saxons leave, their harsh laughter
echoing behind them.
I cannot help it.
A scream, a scream for all the
anguish and fear and hate
is surging up from my chest,
tumbling over itself in its haste to get out,
and I scream and scream, a baby,
an animal.
Gwynivere stares at me in shock.
Her hair, tangled with leaves and
dirt, hangs over her eyes.
What if I led them to Arthur?
To Father and all the people
I have and love in this world?
I am still screaming.
I cannot stop.
Then hands cover my hands,
warm and soft,

like a butterfly's wings.

And the screams stop.

My chest is empty.

Even my heart, my little

sparrow, seems to have left me.

I am bereft and frightened.

Are you — are you all right?

Gwynivere asks, her eyes wide.

Your arm, I mean.

I — I am fine, I mutter.

My throat is raw and

it smarts with each word.

Each breath.

Suddenly my rage is only for her.

What are you doing here?

Why did you follow me? I chastise.

What were you thinking?

I want to hurt her.

Gwynivere turns her head and rests it on her arm.

What was I thinking? she shouts back at me.

I am not the one who got caught.

If you were not so careless, this would
never have happened. But you
follow the men like a pathetic puppy dog.
Why would they ever want to see you? she snarls.
Her words sting, as much as my throat
and the wound on my arm.
But I am grateful for these piercing
breaths, each one a reminder, a gift.

   I live, yet.
Why would they want to see me? I laugh,
disbelieving her arrogance.
I can heal them; when they are wounded,
they look to me! I scream at her.

   How dare she!
They look to you, ha! Her voice and face
are filled with scorn.
But they want to look at me.
Not at young pups, she spits.
I feel as though I have been slapped.
Every time, her slings and insults
assail me anew.

Fool, I mutter.

Yes, I am a fool. But you are a bigger one,
she mocks.

The time creeps past, and the light
outside the tent grows weaker.
Gwynivere grows restless, her legs
twitching and rustling beneath her skirts.
They will not hurt us,
Gwynivere remarks tonelessly.
That Saxon pig is afraid of Arthur.
A savage grin twists her coral lips.
How can you be so certain? I ask.
Because I know men. You're
bleeding all over me, she snaps.
I — I am sorry, I murmur. *It will stop soon.*
We are silent.
She knows men.
She knows how to manipulate men.
This is why Arthur will marry her.
Why Lancelot trails after her

as though he has been enchanted.

Why I shall remain alone.
How can she still be so cruel,
even now, when we are here,
trapped, together?
Yet —
yet, she tried to save me.
The realization gives me a start.
Yes, she tried to rescue me.
When she saw the Saxons seize me,
she flew from the trees like a lioness
protecting her cub.
She does not hate me.
She pretends.
Gwynivere, I begin.
I am sorry. Sorry that you
became entangled in this mess
with me.
She picks up her head and looks at me.
I do believe her eyes soften,
but she does not speak.

The minutes pass slowly, achingly.
My arm continues to bleed, and I
am beginning to feel faint.
My head spins, and my eyes
start to roll back in my head.
Elaine! Gwynivere screams.
Her hands hit mine, and she is
shaking my wrists frantically.
My — *there are some herbs,* I whisper,
leaves in the pouch that
hangs about my neck.
If — *if I lean toward you,*
can you reach it?
I open my eyes and sway sickeningly,
as I try to inch toward Gwynivere,
craning my neck. She wiggles
her hands in their ropes, and reaches
for the tiny leather pouch.
I — *I think I can,* she murmurs,
her brow wrinkled as she pushes as

far forward as she can.

The ropes are straining at her wrists,

biting into the white flesh, but she does

not even flinch.

I have it! she crows happily.

My head feels cloudy,

like I could float away, leave

my body behind, on the floor of this

dirty tent.

Elaine, Gwynivere growls, *Elaine,*

do not faint. Do not! Tell me what to do!

She is shaking me again.

Gwyn — Gwynivere, take the milfoil —

The what? she interrupts. *I do not know*

what that is. There are flowers, leaves

in here. Tell me which one to take!

There is an edge of

mania behind her words.

The milfoil, the feathery green leaves,

those will help the blood to clot.

Do you see it? I am so tired, so weak.
Yes, yes — this? she asks, holding up the
needlelike leaves.
Yes, that is the one, I reply.
Press them into the wound,
here on my arm. I indicate
the knife wound with my chin.
Can you reach? I ask.
Can you move closer to me? she urges.
I slide closer to her, and the scent
of roses stirs me from the sleepy
state I am entering, as I grow
weak from blood loss.
I wince as she prods the
cut, and the leaves fill the wound,
stanching the blood.
Her fingers are surprisingly gentle,
moving quickly and softly,
like a hummingbird.
I bite my lip, teeth sinking into

flesh, as the burning overwhelms
me for an instant, then dulls.
Thank you, I whisper. *That is better.*
And everything goes black.

XXXIII

The sound of quiet weeping
wrests me from my sleep.
As my eyes slowly open, I am
startled to remember where I am,
tied up in a cavelike tent,
Gwynivere bound and beside me.
Her chin is on her chest, and her shoulders
shake with tears.
Gwynivere?
She lifts her head quickly.
You — you are alive! she breathes.
I thought you had died.
And tears fill her cornflower eyes and
course down her cheeks.
*I was so frightened. I thought you had
left me alone,* she says.
I am sorry to have given you a fright,

I tell her. *It is all right. I will live.*
Gwynivere meets my grin with her own,
and we both begin to giggle blackly.
I will live, but who knows for how long?
Silence descends upon us once more.
Darkness has fallen outside, and
the tent is filled with shadows, the
only light coming from a single lantern
near the flaps. The Saxons must have
come while I slept.
I watch the orange flame dance and
flicker. I wonder if my father and brothers
sit beside a fire, too, tonight.
I wonder if they live.
I wonder if I led the Saxons to them.
If they have been slaughtered like sheep,
or if they have already met in combat.
Dread and fear take root in my belly,
growing like a vine up into my chest,
my throat.
I am sure they are quite safe,

Gwynivere breaks into my thoughts.

W-what? I ask.

I am sure your father and brothers are safe,
she responds. *There has not been any fighting
yet. I overheard the pigs talking.*

You can understand them? I ask, incredulous.

*Just bits. There are Saxons living in the
summer lands of my father.*

*But they expect to meet Arthur in battle
in the morning, by the rise
of the sun,* she answers.

How did you know what I was thinking?
I whisper, still shocked by her intuition.

My father is out there too, she replies simply.
And I worry as well.

I am sorry, I whisper. *Of course
you are worried too.*

I wonder if I can begin to know her.
Neither of us speaks, but a question
is burning my tongue.

Why do you hate me? Why have you hated

me since you arrived at Caerleon?
Gwynivere's head snaps up, her
mouth snaps open and closes again.
Then she looks down again,
huddling her knees close to her chest.
I — I do not hate you, she stammers softly.
Then she looks at me directly,
her face regal and eyes frosty again.
You think you are better than everyone.
The way you run around the camp
like a — a heathen. Well, you are not
better. Gwynivere's eyes slant.
A fox, with teeth bared.
I do not think myself better
than anyone, Gwynivere. That is not true,
I reply. *And I think you know it to be false.*
Gwynivere shrugs her shoulders
as though she does not care either way.
And this time the silence is heavy;
it weighs on my shoulders, my aching
arm, and on my eyelids.

293

Soon, my eyes are too heavy to
keep open, and I feel myself drifting
off to sleep. Before they close
a final time, I see Gwynivere is
already asleep.

XXXIV

The hammering of boots
on earth, of sticks on drums,
of swords on shields wakes me.
The drums beat fiercely now,
and tremors ripple through
the ground.
It has begun.
*They have been fighting since
dawn.* Gwynivere's tone is flat,
her eyes flat too.
How far away are they? I ask,
shaking my head, rubbing my
wrists. My hands and arms have
not woken up yet, my injured shoulder
throbs dully.
At least it does not feel inflamed.
I do not know, she replies.

If I cock my head and strain,
I can hear cries of pain and death
riding on the wind.

    Whose are they?
I fight down the panic that rises
from my belly.
But I have witnessed too many
battles to get scared again.
I have listened to too many
war stories to be frightened
by this, the workings of men.
Yet I cannot force the terrible thoughts
from my mind.
What if I never see Lancelot again?
What if I never feel my father's embrace
again? What if I never hear Tirry's
comforting words again? What if I never feel the
tug of Lavain's sly hands on my braids again?
What if I never talk with Arthur again?
Or laugh with Tristan, and feel the glow
of his friendship again?

The tears threaten once more.
I blink to fight them back,
but one slips down my cheek anyway.
You are right, Gwynivere, I was
a fool, I chastise myself.
Such a stupid fool. What did I hope
to achieve? Now I have gotten us
caught, like foxes in a snare,
and Arthur will have to
pay dearly to win us back.
I am so stupid.
He was right. . . .
I am a child.
Suddenly Gwynivere's hands
are on mine.
No, Elaine, do not berate
yourself. Your intentions
were noble, and if you had met
with Arthur's men, you would have
done well to nurse the wounded.
You are brave, while I, I am nothing

but a jealous peahen. I was jealous,
Elaine — that is why I followed you.
She looks down at the floor.
I saw how all the men look on you,
with admiration and as a friend.
All of them — Lancelot, Arthur,
Gawain. No man has ever looked
at me but to see my figure, my face.
I hate them for it. But mostly, I hate
myself, because I am nothing more than
a seashell, beautiful on the outside,
empty within. And that is why
I was so horrid to you.
My heart is beating fast, my
head spinning with disbelief.
Can she really be saying these
things? Can she really be jealous
of me?
Gwynivere, I start, unsure of how
to continue, how to make her see.
Gwynivere, you are beautiful, and

I am jealous of you for that. For the
way the men — the way Lancelot —
looks on you.
She shifts her eyes away, her
brow creasing, her cheeks coloring.
I have loved him since I was a child,
I tell her. *But you are not empty.*
You could not say these words,
you could not believe them, if you were.
What do you know? Gwynivere grumbles.
I know, Gwynivere. I was there when you
leaped from the forest to rescue me.
That did not do us any good, did it?
she mutters scornfully.
But you acted without any care for
your own well-being. You acted to save me,
I remind her.
But I failed. And my life only tells the story
of a woman without a will. Without a spine.
I could not even choose my own husband;
I was simply promised to a

man I had never met, as though
I were a — a horse.
The decision was made for me,
because I am empty. Her lips
are a tight line of resolve.
Gwynivere, may I ask you a question?
She shrugs her shoulders listlessly.
What do you want with Lancelot when
Arthur is so good and kind . . .
and, well, our leader — the one
every man and woman looks to?
Why do you? she hurls the question
back at me.
I do not know, I remark. *But I think it is . . .*
I try to think back to when it began.
Lancelot saved me when I was very young.
I recall that day he came to take Lavain away
to be a soldier, that day in the river,
all the memories of his friendship
floating into view behind my eyes.
One day, I was swimming by

myself in a river, when one of the men
began throwing rocks at me.
I was only twelve years old or so.
But Lancelot appeared and
scared Balin away, and then
he fished me out of the river . . .
and then he asked me to teach him
how to swim. A silly smile has
spread over my face, I realize,
and a warm blush quickly takes its place.
Huh. Well, I cannot have him anyway,
Gwynivere remarks impassively.
We are quiet, and suddenly I
notice that I cannot hear the sounds
of fighting any longer.
Do you think the battle has ended? I ask.
Gwynivere cocks her head and listens,
her brow creased.
No, I do not believe so. The Saxons have
not returned to the camp.
What could have happened to bring about

such quiet? I ask, my heart beating with dread,
as I see a thousand terrible images,
my family, my friends, lying dead
on a bloody battlefield.
Hush, Elaine, Gwynivere soothes,
do not let your mind wander to those
dark places. All will be well, you will see.
She begins to hum a tune,
softly, with such gentleness in her voice,
that instantly the fear and pain are driven from
my mind, and I feel the sparrow has come
back to her nest in my chest,
where she rests peacefully.
Thank you, Gwynivere.
You are good.
Remember that always.
And I feel myself lulled to sleep
once more:

XXXV

The tent flaps are flung open by
a hairy hand, and a hairy
body follows. Yellow Hair's
companion.
Gwynivere jerks her head up.
She had fallen asleep as well.
The Saxon looks at us with a leer
that sends shudders running
down my spine. Streaks of
dried, crusty blood cover his
face and chest, his fingernails,
too, I notice.
He comes to us and kneels.
Gwynivere and I both shrink back
as he bends over us.
But to our surprise, he does
not raise a fist, he does not

appear inclined to violence.
Rather, he begins to untie
our wrists. My heart leaps
with surprise. Perhaps the men
have come to rescue us!
You stay here, the Saxon grunts.
No sound.
No run away.
You prisoners. We take soldiers
and coffers of gold
for you.
That is . . . if Arthur is willing to pay.
His lips curl back in a hideous
laugh that barks and coughs
from his chest.
He shoves a foul and sullied-looking
pan at us.
We watch you. No run away.
No sound, he repeats.
My stomach turns, the smell
of the pan too foul. I

understand it is a kindness
being extended to us. A bedpan
for our use.
He turns, rises, and leaves,
his looming shadow
darkening the outside of the tent,
where he stands guard over us.
Gwynivere and I take turns
moving to the far corner of the
tent to make use of the Saxon's
disgusting gift.
All my joints ache with stiffness.
I look at the wound on my arm.
A brown crust of scab has begun to
grow over the gash.
At least it heals well.
I begin to pace around the tent,
Gwynivere comes to join me.
It feels good to be moving again,
even if only within the confines of
this cage.

There has to be a way to escape, I
murmur to myself.
How? Gwynivere moans. *They
stand outside, guarding us
like a chest of gold.*
She shakes her head, defeated.
*I will not allow us to be traded
for men we know, men I —*
we love, I declare. *It will not happen
as long as I live. I would rather
kill myself.* I am unbending
and resolute.
What do we do? Gwynivere asks.
*I do not know, but I will
think of something,* I tell her.

XXXVI

As dusk falls outside the tent,
we hear the murmuring of voices,
of the Saxons gathered a short
distance from our prison.
Their voices are hushed, but
their rasping words slide through
the night air to our ears.
Can you make out what they are saying?
I ask Gwynivere.
She has been crouching near the entrance
of the tent, brow wrinkled as she
concentrates. But she shakes her head.
No. Their accent is too thick. I know
not the specifics of their discussion.
I am pacing again, like a wolf
trapped in a cage.
There must be a way out,

there has to be.

Suddenly I look at the ground.

At the back of the tent, the skin

hangs a bit loosely, where it

grazes the dirt floor,

not pegged properly with a stake.

What if —

Wait! Gwynivere's voice

is excited.

What is it? I ask,

hurrying to her side.

Listen, she whispers to me.

What do you hear?

I hear . . . our language! I exclaim.

They have a Briton!

My thoughts are racing with my pulse.

Have they captured someone from

Arthur's army? Do they have another

prisoner?

Listen, Gwynivere says again.

Arthur's army is camped by

the River Avon, the strange voice
reveals.
A spy, I breathe.
Yes. Gwynivere nods. *Someone who
knows everything about Arthur's movements,
his plans.*
We have to do something. I say, my panic
returning. *We have to stop him.*
How can we stop him? Gwynivere moans. *We are
trapped in this prison, remember?* Her
face is cloudy. *Shhh, he talks still.*
The spy speaks. *'Round the hill Badon,
to the south lies the River Avon,
by which you arrived here, I believe.*
A Saxon grunts in agreement.
Follow that river, the spy continues,
*and you will find Arthur.
He will never expect you to
come in the night. His men will be
unprepared, they will fall,
easy prey to your battle-axes and swords.*

Go, tonight, the spy spits, his
voice muffled by the rising clamor
of the Saxons.
That is it. We have to warn them, I declare.
I rise and move to the back of the tent.
Our guard is still pacing in front of the
entrance, but there is no shadow at the
back. They have left us an opening.
Gwynivere, come here! I whisper,
motioning her to where I stand.
Look, down here, I instruct her,
and we both kneel, and I show her
where the bottom of the tent
hangs over the ground, unpinned
and loose.
If we dig, I whisper, *we can tunnel
below the tent, escape,
and warn Arthur.*
How can we dig that deep? Gwynivere's
voice is heavy with defeat,
but a glimmer of hope flashes in her eyes.

We have no choice now. We have to
warn them. Please, I am begging you.
Help me, I plead.
She appears frozen, but suddenly
she shakes her head as though
throwing off a veil, and she is
stirred to motion.
All right. Let us dig to freedom.
Our fingers scratch
at the hard-packed earth.
Soon our nails are torn and ragged,
dirt lodged deep in their beds,
but we dig tirelessly, and soon
there is a sizable trough. I can now
slide my arm underneath the bottom
of the tent and dig on the outside.
We stop frequently, as we hear the
Saxons moving about, their voices
coming and going in a rough rumbling.
Our tent must be near the periphery of their
camp, for no one moves outside the back

311

of it, but footsteps pass often
in front of the entrance.
Suddenly we hear our guard
talking with another man.
Yellow Hair.
I recognize his voice.
Quick, throw your shawl
over the hole! I hiss at Gwynivere.
She unties her shawl and covers
the impression we have made in the dirt,
and we slide over to the center support beam,
just as the flaps fly open, and Yellow Hair,
his greasy hair and beard flecked with
ash and bits of food and blood, enters.
His deadened eyes sweep the room,
sweep over us, falling on the shawl
on the ground at the back.
My heart stops, and I can hear
Gwynivere take in a sharp breath.
You are cold, no? he barks
at both of us.

I am so warm from the effort
of our digging, I pray he does
not notice the sheen of moisture on my face,
which is mirrored on Gwynivere's.
You dropped your cloth. He jerks
his chin toward the back of the tent.
I am sitting on my hands
so he does not notice the dirt,
and my nails curl painfully into my fists.
My breath has escaped, my heart
has taken on a wild
beat that must be as audible
as a war drum, and I am certain
he will discover our secret doings.

  Then what will happen?
Hmmf, he grunts, *obedient prisoners*
we have. An evil smile spreads
across his vulture's face, then he turns
and leaves.
I fall down backward, my chest heaving,
my hands shaking.

Gwynivere's head is in her hands.
Oh my God, she whispers. *I thought*
he would take the shawl.
I know. I feared the same!
We smile at each other wildly,
and fall into a fit of giggles.
Shhh, I say, trying to draw a breath
in between bouts of laughter.
We move back to our tunnel,
and begin tearing at the earth again.
The night wears on, and still
we dig, our fingers aching and
trembling from the effort.
Finally I think there is room
enough for us to burrow under
the tent to the other side, to freedom.
A wild urgency drives me;
I have to get to Arthur,
to Tirry and Lavain and Father.
To Tristan.
I have to warn them.

Before it is too late. I touch the beads
hanging around my neck.
Swiftly, my mind diverts
into an unexpected thought —
I think of Tristan, where I
would have expected to think of
Lancelot.
Well, Tristan has been my true
friend these last weeks.
I should not be surprised.
And just as quickly, my mind
flies back to its purpose.
We need a plan, I tell Gwynivere.
What for? she asks. *We just run,
around the mountain, to the south.
As the spy said.*
No! The harshness of my voice
startles both of us. *Only one of us
can go. The other must create a
diversion, so the Saxons do not
realize our purpose. So the other can*

get away. Gwynivere's
eyes widen and a terrified look
crosses her face. I think quickly.
I will escape first, run through the
camp and in the noise and chaos
that is sure to follow me, you
will run in secret. You must
go past the mountain and find the river.
Follow the stars, and you will
find Arthur and warn him,
I decide. *I shall follow, once you*
have had time to get away.
Elaine, they will never let you —
Hush, I cut her off. *Gwyn, there is no*
choice. You must go to Arthur.
But — she begins.
Do not argue with me, I tell her,
putting my hand over hers.
There is no other way.
You must wait until you hear
the noise when they discover me in their

midst. Then count to ten and
run, I command her.
Gwynivere looks at me as though
the sky is falling down upon our heads.
I have never seen such a stricken look
in anyone's eyes.
We grab each other and
embrace.
I will do it, she says, her chin
set with resolve.
Gwyn —
Suddenly tears are streaming
down my face, and my
body is trembling.
Please, tell my father and my
brothers that I am so sorry.
That I love them.
You will tell them yourself,
Gwynivere says, putting her
hands on my shoulders and
giving me a little shake.

I recall my own voice telling
Gwynivere that we have no choice.
Right, I say. Then I beckon for
her to raise the skirt of the tent
as high as possible and I begin
to wriggle on my stomach into
the trench we carved out of the dirt.
The cool night air crashes
over my face, lifting off the
sweat and drying my tears.
As I rise to my feet, I look
all around me.
I was correct in guessing that
our tent was on the periphery of the
camp. All of the tents are arranged
in a circle, the mountain looming at
the far end of the camp. I wiggle
my fingers under the tent,
to let Gwynivere know I am all right.
Remember, I whisper into the
tent's skin, *wait until you hear*

the shouts, and count to ten. Mount Badon
lies on the far side of the camp. I will
lead the men away from there.
Elaine, comes her hushed voice.
Farewell!
My heart stops for a moment,
and I whisper,
O Mistress of the Moon,
O Goddess,
keep her safe,
keep my friend safe
in her purpose.

My friend.
And you, too, my sister!
I call softly.
I press my hand to the wall of the
tent, then turn.
I must attract the Saxons'
attention and lead them away
from the mountain. Then I must
switch courses and run back to the

mountain.

I take a deep breath.

My sparrow is flitting and
dancing in my chest. She swoops and
does loops and circles in my belly.

Give me your wings, I pray.

Another breath.

My hands and legs feel shaky.

One more breath, then I run.

I run, circling the tent, and fly
past the guard. His eyes open
wide and he gives his head a little
shake, as though he cannot believe
what he sees.

Then he drops the cup he was
holding and begins to shout.

He starts to speed after me,
raising his ax and brandishing
it in the air. I cannot look back
at him, I must run and run.

I swerve and weave through the

tents, leading what is now a pack
of Saxon warriors on my heels, south of
the mountain, and they are hollering and
waving their instruments of war at my back.
I am fast, but they are more powerful, with
longer legs. I can feel their hot breath on
my back, the stench of their unwashed
bodies urging my legs on.
I am unaware of breath, of pain.
I feel only the wind at my feet and the heat
of their bodies on my neck.
Run! the wind calls.
Run! I beg of Gwynivere in my mind.
I am darting and weaving like a fox,
but suddenly something whistles past
my ear in a cool rush of air.
I see the white feathers in the moonlight.
An arrow.
Out of the corner of my eye
I spy a figure moving toward
the mountain.

Gwynivere.

Her golden hair streams out

behind her, like one of Arthur's

battle standards.

She goes and no one follows.

I turn and race behind a tent.

Another arrow hurtles past me.

I catch sight of the moon,

half revealed in all her splendor.

Please, please help me, I pray silently.

I look around, but Gwynivere is nowhere

in sight. I change direction and begin to head

for Mount Badon.

In the distance, I can see the sparkle of the moon

glinting off the watery surface of the river.

I can make it, I tell myself.

The Saxons are closing in, and arrows are

now flying as fast as the beat of a

hummingbird's wings.

My legs and my lungs are burning,

but I keep moving.

There is no choice.

I have no choice.
As I round the base of the great hill,
I can see the river curving,
carving through the land just up ahead.
There are dark figures like teeth
or men
looming before me.
My heart sinks with dread.
The Saxons, they must have
guessed our purpose and headed
off Gwynivere, and now they wait for me.
But my legs do not stop moving.
Let them try to take me!
A wild laugh parts my lips,
my mouth is dry and my eyes water.
As I near the river, the dark shapes grow
larger. They are too tall to be people.
Closer now, closer!
My heart beats an angry tattoo.
My own drum of war.

They are not Saxon soldiers after all!
Boats!
I fly toward them, and the intricate
carvings on the stern of the nearest boat
become clear in the moonlight.
What a beautiful vessel,
a beautiful vessel to carry me home!
    Another giggle laced with fear and
    an edge of lunacy.
I run to the craft and begin to push,
willing it to slide into the water.
I turn and drive my back against
the boat's massive weight.
Suddenly there is a hissing sound, and
my mind is stunned as a burning pain
explodes in my body.
I look down and there, lodged in the soft flesh
between my shoulder and my chest, the wooden
shaft of an arrow, silvery feathers tracing
the end.
Like an animal made wild with fear,

I thrust myself against the boat once more,
and it shakes loose and rolls
into the water.
I stagger down the bank
of the river, dizzily brushing aside the
reeds waving in the wake of the boat's
sluggish track.
Somehow, I catch hold of the craft
and roll myself over its side,
careful not to land on the
arrow buried deep in my chest.
Careful not to look down and
see the blood, the blood that is
warm and sticky on my hands, my face,
that now coats the bottom of the boat.
The Saxons have lined up on the shore,
frozen, as if stunned, and watch me
      float away.
The last thing I remember,
before the grey mists
at the edges of my eyes veil

my vision wholly, is thinking
they must believe me dead.
The boat sways and rocks gently,
drifting lazily along
with the river's current.

The moor . . .
the moor is green and pregnant
with clover and wildflowers,
and I feel the feathery grasses
brushing the palms of my hands,
vivid pink and purple flowers and
the sky is a strange shade of green,
without a hint of a storm.
Suddenly my hand is filled with
beads, cool, ivory-colored beads,
with intricate scrolls and knots
etched into them. They fill my hands
and they fill a basket that hangs from
my arm, and somehow I know
I am richer because of them.

Then a wolf with green-golden eyes
and tawny fur comes to stand beside me.
I am not afraid, for the wolf is my friend.
He nudges my hand with a cold nose
then bounds away, and I chase him
through a shiver of silvery birch trees.
As the wolf and I wind between the
slender trunks, the wolf vanishes,
and as I feel I am losing my breath,
my strength sapping away
Tristan steps from behind a tree
and offers his hand. I take it
and suddenly I feel wings beating
at my back, and Tristan and I turn into
a pair of sparrows.

XXXVII

Sometime, when the moon is high overhead,
I wake from a fog-filled sleep and
run my fingers over the arrow.
I have not the strength nor will
to pull it out, but I know I must.
Slowly I wrap my fingers around
the base of the shaft, feeling too
weak even to keep my fingers from
trembling. Then I pull; the
last drops of strength drain from me,
as a pool of dark blood wells
over my chest.
I fumble with the pouch at my neck,
and manage to ease a pinch of calendula petals
free, and place them in my mouth.
I chew weakly, then place the sticky
clump into the hole left by the arrow.

My eyes grow heavy again.
Has Gwynivere reached Arthur?
I wonder hazily. Has she warned the men?
Will I die here, in this Saxon boat?
And darkness envelops me again.

XXXVIII

I still feel the rocking
of the boat and the river.
A faint light buzzes behind my eyelids.
But I cannot open them.
There is a pressure on my chest,
a terrible weight.
Fear is thick in my mouth,
on my tongue, sour and acidic.
I am alone and dying.
The point of light
grown smaller,
ever smaller now,
ever more distant now.
Does she wake?
Her eyes flutter!
  Delirium before death.
Elaine?

My mother calls to me.

Truly, I die.

Elaine! Wake up!

Elaine!

Why would my mother shout at me?

I have not seen her in so many years.

And she shouts at me?

Is she not happy to receive me in heaven?

Elaine!

Mother?

The film of dirt encrusted

on my eyes tears at my lashes

as I force myself to open them.

The soothing motion of the boat stops,

the peace I felt as I slipped away,

into the darkness, fades.

I am not on a boat.

Nor am I dead.

As the world and my life

swim slowly into view,

faces loom against

an overpowering brightness.
I am in a sun-filled tent, and
my father's face, wrinkled,
drawn, and pinched with worry,
grows clear. He kneels
beside my head, and as I look at him
and ask, disbelievingly, *I live?*
a smile widens, smoothing the creases
at his brow and mouth.
Beside him, Lavain sits, his eyes
rimmed in red, as though
he has been weeping.
And Tirry paces behind them, wringing
his hands, his knuckles white,
his face white too.
Tristan sits beside Lavain,
his golden eyes so filled
with fear, his face haggard
and fraught with shadows.
Elaine, he breathes, *thank God.*
Tirry stops pacing and stares at me intensely.

He closes his eyes, his lips
moving in what I guess are words
of silent thanks.
I reach for my father's hand.
It is rough and warm.
Yes, he murmurs, *you live.*
And we live because of you.
What — what happened? I ask,
feeling a drowsiness closing in.
I fight it off and struggle to sit up,
but Lavain gently pushes me
down against the pallet on which
they have laid me.
Do not try to sit up, Lavain says,
his voice so gentle and soft.
I think of small green turtles
on their beds of moss;

       he was gentle then too.
There was a battle.
Arthur's voice startles me,
and I turn to see him standing

beside Gwynivere at the foot of my bed,
his arm just brushing her shoulder.

Gwynivere reached us and told us
of the Saxons' plan to attack us
while we slept; she told us of your —
your deeds.

And we readied for battle, praying
you would return to us, knowing we
fought not just for Britain, but for you,
for your bravery. We fought to honor you.

And we pushed back the Saxons, he says
solemnly, his eyebrows knitted together.

We slaughtered them, Lavain breaks in.

And they ran, ran for their boats and they
will not be back for a very long time.

I look to Arthur, then Tirry and Father,
and they nod solemnly.

You were victorious? I ask wondrously.

We were victorious, Arthur affirms.

And now the dawn of peace
tolls throughout all this land.

I cannot believe it.

Gwynivere did it, our plan worked.

Then I notice Lancelot, lurking

behind Arthur. He catches

me looking at him and looks away.

My father rises to his feet, grasping

Lavain's shoulder for support.

Come, my sons, let us leave her

in peace. She needs to rest.

Tristan comes to stand where

my father was, and looks into my eyes.

I will be back, he whispers gruffly,

and he squeezes my hand then turns

to follow my brothers.

Arthur kneels beside me, then.

His voice is thick. *You will never know*

how grateful to you I am. How much

I admire you.

How proud I am to call you friend.

He straightens. *Your father*

is right, you must rest.
And I do not wish to earn
his ire, nor that of your
diligent nurse, he says,
smiling at Gwynivere.
He presses his lips to my forehead
and goes, the tent flaps rustling behind him.
Gwynivere looks at me anxiously,
and moves to follow Arthur.
But I must speak with her.
Gwyn! I call weakly.
Oh, Elaine! she cries and rushes to my side,
throwing her arms around my neck.
How do you feel? she asks.
Awful, I reply, smiling.
As though an arrow has pierced my chest.
It has, she giggles.
We did it, Gwyn, I whisper in the wilderness
of her thick, flaxen hair.
We did, she agrees, her face
shining with tears. *Elaine,* she begins again,

336

you will be so proud of me.
When Tirry found the hole in your chest,
I knew to put milfoil on the wound, because
there was so much blood —
her face drops, as though a cloud falls over it
— so much blood. But the milfoil
stanched the flow, and then I
used the red clover to draw away
inflammation.
She smiles again, her eyes full of question.
Thank you, I whisper, reaching for her hand.
Thank you for saving me.
It is astonishing how everything is so
different from just one half moon ago.
I have come to care for Gwynivere,
greatly, and she for me.
She squeezes my hand,
as though to say she is filled with the
same wonder.
Gwynivere sits with me awhile longer,
until I tell her I am tired.

When you wake, I will bring you
some broth to sip, she says,
reluctant to leave.
My eyelids grow heavy once again,
and a dreamless slumber descends.

XXXIX

Time moves in strange ways during
these days and nights of my healing.
It slithers like a snake, slippery and sly;
then night falls like a blanket,
muffling and smothering the pain.
The pain moves in strange ways, too,
like the current of the River Usk,
scratchy and warm as silt,
and when I allow myself to remember the
arrow standing out from my chest,
the heavy throbbing overwhelms me,
then it drifts away again, like the
tide beneath a full moon.
My father and brothers come to sit with me,
they hold my hand and sing me
songs of battle and glory.
And they whisper that the glory is mine.

They whisper of the glory of
the Lady of Shalott.

    My glory.
I think of that great oaken loom,
gleaming gold in a patch of sunlight,
and the stories my mother would weave
into her tapestries. When I recover,
I will build myself a new loom and weave
my own story, the story of my family
and my friends, this land
and the glory that we shared.
As long as I must lay flat on my back,
Gwynivere comes each day and
feeds me broth, bringing the spoon
slowly to my lips, allowing me to
sip the warm soup, until my strength
returns and I can sit up.
It is odd to be the patient.
I do not enjoy it, but I use the time
to teach Gwynivere what I know of healing.
She is an eager student, and

she sings me songs, too,
sweet songs of love, and
I notice a change in her. Her face
has softened, and there is a peace
in her eyes.

Gwynivere, you look different, I remark
one day. *Tell me what has happened to you.
Is it Lancelot?* I ask.

No, it is not Lancelot, she replies. *It is
Arthur.* And a smile breaks over her
face like a sunrise. Then her forehead
creases. *Before you returned to us,
before the boat that bore you floated
down the river, into the camp,
when I told Arthur all that we had heard,
and when I told him what you had done,
I saw such a look of fear on his face.
He was so scared, Elaine. Scared for you,
scared for all of us. It was as if all of his beautiful
humanity was revealed in that singular expression
of fear and love. And at that moment,*

I think, I began to love him.

Her face is radiant.

I did not choose him, in the beginning,

but that night, she pauses to draw a breath,

that night I made a choice, and it was

the right one. When Arthur returned from

battle, he and I spoke

as we watched over you.

He told me that I did not have to marry him

if I did not want to. He told me —

he told me it was for me to decide.

In that moment, I knew. I knew that he

and I were meant for each other.

Her smile widens, and in this moment,

she truly looks like an

enchanted faerie queen.

XL

When next I wake, a crawling
itch prickles my back, and I
wriggle around on
my pallet, trying to reach it.
A searing pain blazes a path
from my chest to the crown
of my head and I am thrust
back down on the bed
by the white hot fury of it.
A small cry escapes from
my lips, and suddenly the tent
flaps are flung open, and
Tristan flies to my side.
What is it, Elaine? he asks,
his face a mask of worry.
Hello, I try to say, but my throat
is parched and the word gets stuck.

Shhh, he hushes me, and lifts
a mug of water to my lips. *Drink this
and lie back.*
I am fine, really, I argue.
What happened? he asks,
his golden eyes narrowing.
It is nothing, I reply, shifting
uneasily. *Just some pain. I am
quite well. Were you — were you listening
outside the tent?* I ask.
A scarlet blush colors his
cheeks. *I — your father asked me
to keep watch to make sure you
were all right,* he murmurs,
looking down.
I see, I say. *Well, now that you are here,
how will you entertain me?* I ask,
smiling at my friend.
Entertain you? he asks. *Am I nothing more
than a court jester?*
Exactly. I smile. *And I the queen.*

Tristan's hair grows long, curling
in tawny locks about his ears,
touching his shoulders.
His eyes are like a forest
floor mottled by pools of
sunlight, sparkling with mirth, and his
face opens in a slow, easy smile.

He is quite handsome, I think.
Let me see, Tristan says, sitting
beside the pallet. *How can I
entertain you? Perhaps, rather
than a jester, a bard might do?*
I nod my head, looking forward
to hearing him sing.
Tristan sings to me of a knight
who has lost his lady love,
and as he slays dragons and giants,
this knight can only think of getting back
to the lady who holds his heart,
to the lady who waits for him.
I close my eyes, and

his low, reedy voice summons
moonlight and the sweet scent of
leaves and earth. The heady
perfume of lilies and rose gardens.
How long it has been since I
have stepped inside a garden. . . .
When the song ends,
he looks at me for a long while
in silence. Then, he whispers,
Have I entertained you well,

my lady?
His gaze is intent, as though
he searches for something
hidden behind my eyes.
The way he looks at me makes
it hard to breathe.
Tristan, I start, unsure of what I
want to tell him.
Somehow, in this moment,
I feel our friendship has taken
a turn, an inexplicable change

of direction, and I know not where
it leads.

Thank you, I finish.

He leans down and brushes
his lips over my forehead.

Sleep well, and dream of pleasant things.

I am happy to see you wear the necklace.

He grins, then, as I watch his back
retreat from the tent,

I cannot help but think of the strange
dream of the wolf that came to me,
that haunted me, as I lay dying
in the Saxon boat.

XLI

Arthur has decided that we
will return to Caerleon-on-Usk.
The men move around this camp,
rolling up tents, packing away
the instruments of war.
Gwynivere sits with me while
the men are busy, and when it is time
to go, she helps me gently from my bed.
I have not taken a step in five days,
and my legs are weak, and they tremble
and threaten to collapse with each step.
Gwynivere cannot abide my weight, and
she bids me to sit, while she calls for
one of my brothers to help her.
Lavain thunders into the tent,
his eyes flashing.
It is too soon, he storms. *She should not*

be taking this journey now.
Lavain, I am right here, so you
need not speak as though I were not,
I scold him gently.
And, besides, I am perfectly capable
of making this journey.
My brother looks down at the
ground abashedly.
Very well. His voice is still gruff,
but gentler now.
Carefully he lifts me from the pallet.
Are you all right? Does it hurt much?
he asks, his face filled with worry.
I want to stroke his cheek and reassure
him, but I remember that this is my
brash brother, and refrain.
I am all right, I tell him.
As we move into the brilliant
sunlight, and into line
behind the others, Lavain holds
my elbow, his other arm wrapped

around my waist.
We walk slowly,
so slowly,
and then
Lavain laughs.
What? Am I too clumsy, too slow?
Perhaps there is a cart I could ride in?
Lavain grins and says, *That is not why I laugh.*
I suddenly remembered when we were young,
how you always insisted on playing on the
stones in the middle of the river
by Shalott. You would step so gingerly
over those slippery rocks, and I was so
afraid you would fall in and be carried
off by the current. Ever I walked beside you,
as slowly as we go now. And you would skip
gaily from stone to stone, singing and
chattering busily to the fish and the trees
and the reeds on the shore.
You would even chatter to me,
talking nonsense and squeezing my hand

with your tiny little fingers.
He pauses and the smile runs away
from his face.
Elaine, do you know how hard it
is not to hold your hand and guard
you still as you step into danger even now?
Ah, Sister, you must take better care.
And he grins again, and this time
I do put my hand to his rough, unshaven
cheek.
Lavain, I begin, a wicked smile on my lips,
if I had known, all these years, that
you still felt inclined to watch over me,
I likely would have been one hundred times
wilder and one thousand times more willing
to seek out danger.
Devil! he cries. And we both laugh,
until I stagger from the pain in my chest
and gasp for breath.
Come, give me no cause to worry more,
he says, trying to hold in his laughter,

and we continue on this way, joking
and teasing as we did when our
greatest concerns were mud pies
and small, green turtles.

XLII

We have walked for several hours
already this day. The sun
soars high overhead, and the
air is warm.
Someone at the front of the company
whistles shrilly, and we halt and
fumble for our skins of water.
There is a small brook some steps
away, and a lovely weeping willow
tree sweeps over it, her branches trailing
in the burbling water.
My chest aches dully, and I make up my mind
to sit for a few minutes in the shade
and fill my skin.
This moment of rest is welcome.
I watch the water skipping over
rocks and swirling in tiny eddies

around the graceful branches.
The willow's boughs
curve in elegant swoops,
and it feels as though she means
to protect me.
Suddenly a shadow crosses
into my pool of shade.
Lancelot, I say, looking up, surprised.
He has avoided me since I came
to the camp by the River Avon.
And now that he approaches,
I recall, with surprise,
how unbothered I have felt
by his absence.
His forehead is creased,
and his emerald eyes rove
across my face, as though searching
for something.
May I sit beside you? he asks hesitantly.
Of course, I answer, shifting to
make room for him to lean against the

furrowed bark of the willow's trunk.

My friend, he whispers, *can you ever*
forgive me?

His eyes are haunted.

He does not give me a chance to speak.

I thought — I thought I would never
see you again. I thought I would never
be able to tell you how deeply sorry I am
for the cruel words I flung at you that
day — that day on the moor. His
voice trembles and breaks.

I think I always knew you — you
loved me, he says. *But I always saw*
you as the small girl who arrived
at camp so many years ago, terrified
and dirty, with great big eyes that
had seen something terrible. You were
always that small girl who learned to
laugh again and to run races
and swim with the fish, and who
looked at me like I was a hero.

He takes a deep breath.

And I loved being your hero.

But that day, that day when you

offered yourself to me, I was

shocked, and I was angry with the

world, drowning in self-pity.

I dismissed you as a child

who could never understand.

But now, I suspect you understood

better than anyone.

A bitter smile that does not

reach his eyes twists his mouth.

Yes, Lancelot, I respond, *I do understand.*

But let us put it behind us now.

Do you forgive me? he asks,

his eyes drowning in sorrow.

Lancelot, you have been my

dearest friend since I was a child.

You have been my knight and, yes, my hero.

And I loved you. But I loved you

when I was just a child.

356

Of course I forgive you.

The lines on his face smooth with relief.

But, Lancelot — I am not sure how

much I may say to him. *You are*

in love with her, still?

He nods slowly. *Yes, I love her,*

but it is hopeless. I know that,

and I will live with it for the rest of my days.

I am sorry, Lancelot, I murmur,

brushing his hand with mine.

I am sorry as well, he says, his

eyes filled with regret.

For so many things.

He sits with me awhile longer,

telling me jokes and recounting

his and Arthur's heroics during

the battle. *And Tristan fought*

with a mighty sword, indeed,

he says, his eyes widening slightly

with surprise. *I have never seen him*

fight so ferociously. As though

a spirit chased him at his heels,
he cut through the enemy as if
he did not even see them. As if he
were possessed by some ghostly force
outside himself. It was a sight to behold.
He grows thoughtful and glances at me.
He tugs a loose lock of my hair.
Perhaps I know
who that spirit was after all. . . .
Well, he shakes himself and stands up.
I shall leave you in peace to rest.
I have a feeling more visitors will follow.
He kneels again and lifts my hand
to his mouth, where he plants
the softest kiss.
A funny grin lifts his mouth. *Be well, Elaine,*
dearest friend of my own heart.
You be well, too, Lancelot, I call after his
retreating back.

How badly I wanted to grow up,
to be a woman, that he might notice me.
But now, now I am happy to enjoy
whatever granule of ease or freedom
I may find,
after all that has happened.
The freedom of childhood innocence.
The freedom of the sparrow.

XLIII

As we prepare to move again, Lavain
has found a horse for me to ride.
He raises me onto the back
of a beautiful roan mare, who steps gently
and saves my poor brother from continuing
on at a snail's gait.
I concentrate on ignoring the pain,
on not falling out of the saddle.
Suddenly Tristan is beside me,
a stormy look in his eyes.
Are you well? he practically shouts.
I nod, startled by his brusque manner,
and he rides ahead without
even a glance back at me.
What bothers him? I wonder.
But I have not the strength to follow him.
When we stop next,

Lavain helps me to dismount,
gently easing me from the roan's back.
He leads me to a resting spot he has found,
beneath a rowan tree.
As I lean back against
the smooth grey trunk,
a shadow crosses into the
cool circle of shade.
Tirry! I exclaim gladly.
How are you faring, Sister?
he asks, kneeling to pat my shoulder.
I am quite well, I reassure him.
He lays a gentle kiss on my cheek,
then rises to report my welfare to
our father.
As I close my eyes to rest,
I feel a shadow fall over me.
I do not look up, expecting
Lavain has returned to bother me more
with his clumsy attempts
at nursing.

You are back so soon? I ask playfully.
Really, I am perfectly —
I expect you mean your knight? No,
I am not he, an angry voice interrupts.
Tristan! I exclaim.
Disappointed? he asks, his
voice brimming with rancor.
Tristan, are you angry with me? I ask,
confused by his tone and the fiery
look in his eyes. *Have I done something
to upset you?*
No, Elaine — you do nothing! His voice
catches on the last word. He throws
himself onto the ground beside me,
but looks down, and directs his body
away from me.
His fingers tear at the grass fiercely.
*Has the earth upset you? Did the grass
give you an itch?* I try to make my voice
light, hoping that gentle teasing will
bring back the easygoing friend I recognize.

I see nothing to laugh at, he spits.
What did Lancelot say to you? More blades
of grass murdered by his hand,
beheaded and drowned in the brook.
What did Lancelot say to me? I repeat,
not understanding what could have made
him so agitated, but starting to
feel irritated by his tone.
What are you talking about? I snap.
Then, I realize, he must have seen me
speak to Lancelot during our last stop.
Lancelot and I had —
matters to discuss.
What matters? Tristan storms.
Tristan, what is it you are getting at?
Lancelot and I had a private discussion
and it is really none of your concern
what we spoke of, I shout, losing my
patience with his ill-tempered tirade.
So, you are in love, then? The cords
in his neck stand out

and his normally bronze face
has turned purple. We do not even have
dyes for our wool that color.
I tell him so.
I should have refrained.
Tristan explodes.
He is a careless ass, and you are
an even bigger fool if you think that
he could love you as much as —
He clamps his mouth shut
and crosses his arms over his chest,
kicking his feet, scuffing the turf, and
glaring at the wide blue sky.
Tristan, I do not love Lancelot, I tell him simply,
nor does he love me.

His words begin to sink in.
I feel a sense of breathlessness.
As much as what? I ask.
Tristan, as much as what?
Tristan whips his head around to look at me.
His green-gold eyes are so serious.

What? he storms. *You have loved him*
all these years and today you stop?
I am so confused by the swinging
pendulum of his temper. But
suddenly, suddenly everything
makes sense. The dream . . .
the dream I had in the boat,
when I was unconscious.
It was all leading to this,
this moment, these feelings.
He is the one.
Tristan is the one.
I want to leap up and sing.

I have to tell him, I realize.
How do I tell him?
How do I make him see?

Have I already lost him?
Fear seizes me, and I begin talking,
words just falling out my mouth,
stumbling over themselves to get out,
to explain, to tell him everything.

I do not think I knew what true love
was, I begin.
Tristan's cat eyes burn into my own,
and a strange feeling dances
through my belly.
But, I believe, I continue, *I know now*
what true love is — *or what*
it should be.
What should it be? Tristan asks,
his voice soft now.
It should begin with friendship, I think.
Suddenly I cannot look at him.
It should begin with friendship and truly knowing
who a person is, knowing his flaws and hopes
and strengths and fears, knowing all of it.
And admiring and caring for — *loving*
the person because of all those things.
Tristan, all these years I was a silly girl
who thought she loved a man who
played with her and plied her with
attention, who made her feel

grown up. But I did not love Lancelot.
I know that now, I explain.
Truly? he asks.
Yes, I tell him, still unable
to meet his gaze.
I feel my face heated by a blush,
and the peculiarity of feeling
this way around Tristan,
who has always been my friend,
makes my heart beat faster, my breath
harder to catch.
I thought I had lost you, Elaine,
he says earnestly. *When Gwynivere*
arrived in the camp that night,
that awful night, she was shaking
and covered with mud and brambles,
and she told us, his voice breaks, *she told*
us what you had done, and I thought
you were gone from me forever.
Then when the fighting began I
could only see your face, and I

hacked through lines of Saxons,
thinking only of you and praying
that you lived. I did not hear the
ringing of my sword on ax or shield,
I heard only your voice and
the sound of your laughter.
And when the fighting ended,
and one of the men spotted an unmanned
boat drifting down the river, I wanted
to believe it carried you back to me,
I wanted to believe it, but I was so
scared. He is trembling forcibly now,
and I take his hand, letting my fingers
stroke the calluses and cuts
and bruised flesh of his palm.
Tristan continues,
All of us, your brothers and father,
Arthur, Gwynivere, Lancelot, Gawain,
all of us, we ran down to the river,
and there you were,
lying in that boat, with that

red rose covering your chest —
only it was no flower. Blood.
He stops to wipe a tear from
his eye, and my heart is beating
so fast, the little sparrow fluttering
her wings so fast.
You were so pale, he goes on,
so white, like death. Yet, so beautiful,
so beautiful it broke my heart.
We all thought you dead.
And your father and brothers were
broken, Lavain fell to the ground,
and I —
He stops for a breath again.
Lancelot and I pulled you from
the boat and we — *we saw the arrow.*
You had pulled it from your own . . . He stops and
starts again. *Then we carried you into the tent,*
and as we lay you down, I felt your breath
on my ear, so weak, so slight.
Like a baby bird's.

But you lived!

He wipes away more tears.

*You lived, and Gwynivere took
control, ordering Lavain to
press on the wound to keep
it from bleeding, and when he did
such a moan of anguish flew from your lips,
my heart broke again. But Gwynivere
stopped the bleeding with the herbs in
that pouch you always wear, and we waited,
all of us, your father and brothers, Gwynivere,
Arthur, Lancelot, and I, in the tent, and all of the
men, every last one of them outside,
and we waited, waited for you to wake up.
And when you opened your eyes,
it was the gladdest moment of my
life. And in that instant, I knew . . .*

His hand tightens around mine.

You knew what? I ask softly.

*I knew that cursed love would never
find me again. I was so frightened*

of love, of falling again, and I tried
to keep away from you, to keep from
thinking of you, and when I
could not, I told myself . . . His
jaw twitches. *I told myself that*
it was not love. I could not love again.
And, besides, you loved another.
But . . . now I know, no love potion could
beget a love this true. For,
I have found the truest love of all
in our friendship.

The heaviness on my chest dissolves.
You love me? I ask.
Elaine, you are the bravest,
the kindest and most beautiful,
person I have ever known. Yes,
I love you. I will love you
for the rest of my life.
His cat eyes hold me in their gaze.
I cannot look away.

The question is, he starts, *can you*
ever love me back?
My breath is hard to catch.
      This is the moment.
      I love him.
Yes, Tristan, my dearest one, I love you.
Always.
I think I have always loved you.
Such a look of relief and joy washes
over his beautiful face, a laugh
erupts from my mouth,
and I bite my lip as it summons back
the throbbing pain in my chest.
My love, he utters so softly,
and takes me in his arms,
clasping me to his chest,
as gently as one would a
bird, and his lips find mine,
in the sweetest kiss.
My head spins and my
belly fills with warm light.

This kiss is more perfect than
I could ever have imagined.
My sparrow, she flickers and wakes
and sings and sings.
A beautiful song of love.

XLIV

We have reached Caerleon-on-Usk at last.
Morgan is there to greet us.
Hello, little one, she murmurs, as she
embraces me. *I see much has happened,
much has changed. And your part to play
was no small one.*
She smiles broadly and extends her hand.
I take it and follow her to her tent,
where she brews a pot of tea.
How is your wound? she asks.
Which one do you mean? I joke.
*At times I feel like one of the
hay targets the men use to
practice their battle skills,
with so many holes poked in me.*
Morgan grins, but her expression
quickly turns stern.

Let me see both of your injuries.
As I unwrap the bandages around
my arm and my chest, her
eyes lighten, and she nods,
looking pleased. *Ah, Gwynivere*
has done well, tending to you.
These will both heal nicely.
I wonder how Morgan knows so much.
Giving voice to my question, she answers,
simply, *I see many things.*
I know that whatever magic she
has, it is not for me to understand.
My place is here, on this land.
It is my magic and my home.
You have done great things,
Morgan says with a tender smile,
and I am so proud of you. And you
have been rewarded with
the greatest riches of all.
I nod, picturing Tristan's lazy grin
and gleaming eyes and remembering

the warmth of his kiss.
What will happen now? I ask.
Will everyone scatter?
I imagine many will return
to the homes they left behind, to their
own families and loved ones, she replies
slowly, *but we will learn more tonight,*
for Arthur has asked everyone
to come to the Round Table.

As the sun sinks in a fount
of crimson, rose, and purple,
Tristan and I begin to make
our way to the Round Table.
We pause, when we reach the copse
of birch trees, and stand among the
silvery trunks.
Tristan wraps his arms around my waist.
My love, he murmurs against my hair.
We should always live among the trees
and grasses and wildflowers, he whispers.

They suit you. I smile in response
and reach up to the nearest branch,
my fingertips grazing the feathery leaves.
Yes, I sigh, *we should always live among the trees.*
As we move toward the Round Table, several
men are stoking a roaring bonfire.
Flecks of white ash fly overhead,
arching toward the heavens.
For an instant I think of the snowy
ashes of our home on Shalott, that night
so long ago, and I shiver.
Then Tristan takes my hand and squeezes it,
and the dark memory is banished.
We sit near Lavain, Tirry, and my father,
near Arthur, Gwynivere, Lancelot, and Morgan.
I know I have earned my place at the Round Table,
and the knowledge makes me glad.
Soon platters of venison and rabbit
and flagons of mead
are being passed around the table.
The mood is light, and

a current of excitement
hovers in the air.
Men speak of going home,
of reunions with wives and sons and daughters,
of land they will farm, of livestock to raise.
Laughter and jokes fill the air,
and we eat and drink until all are stuffed.
Then, as though he steps
out of the very night,
the Merlin appears.
He looks less like a wraith,
but a man of enchantment and vision,
wrapped in a cloak woven of dreamstuff.
His eyes are fierce, but his mouth turns up
in a smile. He takes a seat
on Arthur's left, beside Morgan.
As he sits, all chattering and rustling stops.
All is still.
Arthur rises from his seat and
throws his hands into the air.
Britons! Bravest Britons!

You have won back your land,
wrested her from the grasp of the enemy.
Now she is yours, to live in,
in freedom and in peace.
Arthur's face grows thoughtful.
And he turns to look at each of us in turn,
his eyes lingering on my own.
I smile at him.
He returns my grin with a wide one, then
continues, *I thank you for your service,*
indeed, I will think on each of you
with everlasting gratitude and admiration.
Your deeds have been noble,
your hearts righteous,
and your just reward is due.
Return to your homes, to your families,
and to your farms. Make them vibrant and strong,
and reap all the glory and gifts this
land has to give. But,
for those of you who have lost
so much, for those of you who have

not homes nor wives to return to,

I offer you a choice.

A choice to stay and to

build something new,

something magnificent.

This day, I ask you to join me,

to join me on a new journey:

In this place, on this land,

where the path to our

freedom began, I aim to

build a monument to liberty and peace.

A haven, where

justice will reign as king.

Where any man or woman may

come in search of relief,

in search of redress, when

someone or something

steals away their freedom,

plunders their peace.

Arthur rises and his voice thunders
over the Round Table,

Britons!
Who will stand with me?
Who will stand with me to
build this haven for justice?
Who will stand with me to build
Camelot?

Tristan and I look at each other
and smile. Then, together,
hands entwined, we rise.
And Lavain and Tirry and my father rise.
And Gwynivere stands beside Arthur,
her eyes shining as she stares up at him,
love filling her gaze.
And Gawain and his brothers rise.
And one hundred other men rise.
All are smiling at the prospect of
a future filled with hope.
And finally, Lancelot stands,
but the joy in his eyes is dimmed
as his gaze alights on Gwynivere

clutching Arthur's arm.

     A brewing storm.

My friends, Arthur calls out,

my friends, I thank you. And I welcome

you on this journey.

To peace! To freedom!

To freedom! we cry. *To freedom!*

That night, after the embers have died

and the only light comes from the moon,

I walk among the birch trees,

     a shiver of

       silver silent ghosts.

So long I wanted to grow up

to be a woman,

all the while fighting

the trappings of womanhood.

But now I may be woman

and child and Briton,

and nothing can imprison me again.

I look up to the full moon and whisper,

Lady of the Moon,
for keeping safe all that is dear to me,
for preserving those I love
and this land,
I thank you.

And at that moment,
a lilting melody lifts to the moon as
a single sparrow sings.

Author's Note

I cannot remember the first time I discovered the stories of King Arthur. I have been reading — and loving — them forever, it seems. The legends of King Arthur and his Knights of the Round Table have always been among my favorites to hear, watch, and read. Yet, as I've read more and delved deeper into this incredibly rich and terribly vast canon, the more I have wanted to learn about the history — the true story, if you will — of this king named Arthur.

He is one of the most celebrated literary figures of all time; Arthur and his knights have inspired hundreds of poems, stories, books, plays, and movies — from Sir Thomas Malory's *Le Morte D'Arthur* to Monty Python's *Spamalot* — spanning centuries. As omnipresent and popular as the literature is, I was surprised to discover that there is no hard proof that Arthur actually existed.

Many archaeologists, historians, scholars, and fans have made it their life's work to try to uncover the mystery of

Arthur. There are a multitude of theories, but no hard evidence has ever been brought to bear either way.

As I thought about how to approach writing *Song of the Sparrow*, I knew I wanted the setting and characters to feel authentic, and so I looked back at many texts for guidance, which are listed in the *Suggestions for Further Reading* section.

If the man whom we know as Arthur did live, it was most likely close to the end of the fifth century or during the early sixth century, in what is referred to as the Dark Ages. Approximately three hundred years later, a Welsh monk and historian named Nennius, who, it is believed, had access to fifth-century texts that have since been lost, seems to have left the most promising clue. He writes about Arthur in his *Historia Brittonum*, or *History of the Britons*, casting him as a star military captain:

> Then Arthur along with the kings of Britain fought against them
> in those days, but Arthur himself was the military commander [*dux*
> *bellorum*]. . . . The twelfth battle was on Mount Badon in which there

fell in one day 960 men from one charge by Arthur; and no one struck them down except Arthur himself, and in all the wars he emerged as victor.[1]

While this sounds like proof enough of Arthur's existence, certain glaring exclusions of his name from other earlier texts that date closer to what would have been Arthur's lifetime indicate that perhaps this wasn't the case after all.

A sixth-century British monk named Gildas, who also recorded the history of the Britons, failed to mention Arthur's name even once in his text, *Concerning the Ruin of Britain.* Nor did another historian and clergyman known as the Bede, who wrote a comprehensive work titled *The Ecclesiastical History of the English People* in A.D. 731.

It wasn't until the twelfth century, more than four hundred years after Nennius introduced Arthur, that the mythic king reappeared in the history books. This time, it was a

[1]from the *Historia Brittonum,* http://www.fordham.edu/halsall/basis/nennius-full.html

bishop named Geoffrey of Monmouth who wrote at length about Arthur in his *History of the Kings of Britain.* Geoffrey placed Arthur directly in the line of British kings. He was the first to do so, and it was Geoffrey's writings that spawned the Arthurian legends readers know now.

And so, despite differing accounts and much ambiguity, there are a few things we can say about Arthur with some certainty. The roots of his story lay in the Roman Empire, which was founded circa 31 B.C., and stretched from Rome all the way into northern Africa, parts of Asia, and most of Europe, lasting for nearly fifteen hundred years.

In A.D. 44, the Romans invaded Britain and ruled there relatively peacefully and prosperously for nearly four hundred years. But, in the early fifth century, the Roman Empire began to suffer from rebellions and fighting in its various territories, and Britain itself had also become subject to waves of invasions. The Roman legions that were posted on that remote isle were too few to fend off the growing numbers of invaders, and the soldiers began to rebel. Finally, in A.D. 410, the Roman soldiers and governing officials withdrew from Britain to aid in the fighting in other parts of the Empire, leaving the tiny island completely drained of its former glory and military strength.

The Britons who remained behind lived in small groups, or clans, led by local chieftains. Left to fend for themselves, they fought *among* themselves, as well as against their many enemies. The Britons faced the Picts, tribesmen from what is now eastern and northeastern Scotland, who were called such because of the Latin word *picti*, meaning "painted," as the Picts were said to have tattooed their bodies. Hadrian's Wall, which ran seventy-three miles across the width of Britain, was constructed by the Romans to keep the Picts out of Britain proper. Other enemies of the Britons at this time were the Scots, invaders who came from what is now known as Ireland — the name originates from the Roman name for the Irish, meaning "raider" or "bandit" — as well as the Saxons, from what is now Germany and parts of the Netherlands, who also posed constant threats to Britain at this time.

About forty years after the Roman withdrawal, around A.D. 450, a British chieftain called Vortigern invited a band of Saxon mercenaries into Britain, to aid him in fighting off the Picts. Rather than help defend the land, however, these mercenaries simply paved the way for fleets of Saxon soldiers to enter and devastate the British isle. Ambrosius Aurelius, a British military commander, whom Gildas, Nennius, and Geoffrey of Monmouth refer to as a "King of the Britons," avenged the destruction of Britain by assassinating Vortigern and taking over the leadership of the British forces around A.D. 490. But the Saxons, Picts, and Scots continued to pummel the island, eventually murdering Aurelius, as well.

But this is where certainty leaves off, and it falls to the writers and movie directors and composers to imagine what might have been. There are elements that recur in Arthurian legends that are familiar to many readers — Camelot, the Merlin, Gwynivere, Lancelot, just for starters — and one might wonder, as I did, whether they truly existed. No one knows if Arthur's castle at Camelot or the famed Round Table ever really stood or where, but the archaeologists have all kinds of theories, stretching from Colchester to Cadbury, both towns in England. Whatever the case, though, Camelot and the Round Table have remained throughout the centuries as symbols of peace, justice, and equality.

Interestingly, the Merlin has his roots in ancient Welsh lore. A mysterious character called Myrddin, who prophesizes, can be found in many early texts, as well as ancient Welsh poetry, which was passed down orally. Geoffrey of Monmouth also wrote of the Merlin extensively, as though he indeed were a historical figure. Yet, there is no evidence to suggest that he truly existed.

Nor do we know if Gwynivere lived. It is rumored that in 1191 a grave was found at the Cathedral of Glastonbury, which, according to legend, is in the same spot as the mythical Avalon would have been. The grave was said to contain the skeleton of a very tall man and a petite woman, covered by a cross of lead with an inscription that read "Here lies buried the renowned King Arthur in the Isle of Avalon." However, the cross has been lost to time, as was the grave. But we can speculate: Was that Gwynivere buried with her husband?

Furthermore, there is no evidence that a knight of the

Round Table named Lancelot actually existed, either. In fact, the story of Lancelot's illicit love for Queen Gwynivere has its roots in the earlier tale of doomed love, *Tristan and Isolde.*

And finally, Elaine. She has been present in poems and stories for ages, in various incarnations and in slightly differing circumstances from text to text. In *Le Morte D'Arthur,* she is the daughter of an old knight who gives shelter to Lancelot. Elaine falls in love with Lancelot and begs him to love her back. But he cannot, and so she dies of a broken heart. In the nineteenth century, the British poet Alfred, Lord Tennyson, wrote a long poem about her, titled, "The Lady of Shalott," in which she lives in a tower, under the narrow and lonely strictures of a mysterious curse. The lady cannot look out her window or leave her tower, and so she watches the goings-on outside indirectly through a mirror's reflection. One day, Lancelot passes by, and she glimpses him in the mirror. She falls in love with him immediately; then, unable to stop herself, turns to look at him directly through the window. Suddenly the curse falls upon her, and the window and mirror shatter. The lady knows the end has come, and she runs outside, leaps into a boat, after painting her name on the bow, and dies, sailing downriver to Camelot.

Though Elaine of Ascolat, or the Lady of Shalott as she is more popularly known, is a pervasive figure in literature, there is nothing to suggest such a girl truly lived.

Yet, *none* of this actually matters. These stories, the myth of King Arthur and his companions, live on and persist throughout time because they deal with such incredibly important and universal, such fundamentally *human* themes as love, friendship, loyalty, justice, faith, peace, and hope. And they resonate with the eternal chimes of truth, regardless of history or fact.

I was thrilled to have the opportunity to make a contribution to this canon, to write about my favorite characters, and only recently aware of the latest scholarship, I was excited to try to endow the legend with a historical edge. But I also wanted to try to change something: As I read more and more stories about Arthur and his companions, and as I began studying Arthurian lore in college, I started to notice that the girls and women in these stories were not always treated very kindly. At best, it seemed to me, they were damsels in distress who needed a man to rescue them, and at worse, they were chaperones of doom and destruction. This did not seem fair to me.

And so, I aimed to humanize the characters, to really scrutinize them with a twenty-first-century magnifying glass and imagine how they might actually have related to one another. As I imagined Elaine, who truly has suffered at the hands of male writers, I wanted to give her strength and power and relevance. And indeed, it is without a sword that she manages to save her friends and loved ones.

I have always loved the romance and chivalry that fill the Arthurian stories, but the ideals of freedom and equality and justice are what truly make this mythology so important — and continually resonant. The stories of Arthur and his knights have given centuries of readers hope — hope for peace, and I can only wish that readers of this book take away the same hope.

Lisa Ann Sandell

NEW YORK CITY, 2006

Suggestions for Further Reading

Ashe, Geoffrey. *The Discovery of King Arthur*. New York: Henry Holt and Company, LLC, 1985.

Churchill, Winston Spencer. *The Birth of Britain: A History of the English-Speaking Peoples, Volume I*. New York: Barnes & Noble Books, 2005. (Original publisher: London: Dodd, Mead & Company, Inc., 1956.)

De Troyes, Chrétien. *Arthurian Romances*. Translated by William W. Kibler. London: Penguin Books, 1991. (Written in the second half of the twelfth century.)

Gildas. *De Excidio Britanniae*. Medieval Sourcebook: Gildas: from *Concerning the Ruin of Britain (De Excidio Britanniae)*. http://www.fordham.edu/halsall/source/gildas.html

Hibbert, Christopher. *The Way of King Arthur*. New York: ibooks, 1969 and 2004.

Malory, Sir Thomas. *Le Morte D'Arthur*, The Winchester Manuscript. Oxford: Oxford University Press, 1998. (Written in 1470.)

Monmouth, Geoffrey of. *The History of the Kings of Britain*. Translated by Lewis Thorpe. London: Penguin Books, 1966. (Written between 1129 and 1151.)

Nennius. *Historia Brittonum*. Medieval Sourcebook: Nennius: *Historia Brittonum, 8th Century*. http://www.fordham.edu/halsall/basis/nennius-full.html

About the Author

LISA ANN SANDELL is a writer living in New York City. She is the author of *The Weight of the Sky*, a novel in verse, which was nominated to the American Library Association's 2007 Best Books for Young Adults list. Please visit her website at: *www.lisaannsandell.com*